THE NURSE'S WAR

BOOK 1 IN THE VICTORIA'S WAR SERIES

FENELLA J MILLER

Boldwood

First published in 2015 as Victoria's War: Shadows. This edition first published in Great Britain in 2024 by Boldwood Books Ltd.

Cover Design by Colin Thomas

Cover Photography: Colin Thomas

A CIP catalogue record for this book is available from the British Library.

Paperback ISBN 978-1-83518-663-3

Large Print ISBN 978-1-83518-662-6

Hardback ISBN 978-1-83518-661-9

Ebook ISBN 978-1-83518-664-0

Kindle ISBN 978-1-83518-665-7

Audio CD ISBN 978-1-83518-656-5

MP3 CD ISBN 978-1-83518-657-2

Digital audio download ISBN 978-1-83518-660-2

Boldwood Books Ltd
23 Bowerdean Street
London SW6 3TN
www.boldwoodbooks.com

In memory of my mother, Patrica Cross, nee Rikh, whose memoirs inspired this book.

AUTHOR'S NOTE

The characters in this story are an accurate reflection of the time they are living in. As such, their thoughts, speech and actions are normal for this era. Thankfully we now live in a more enlightened time.

PART I

SHADOWS

1

INDIA – 1938

The night before the long-anticipated trip to Delhi, Victoria's mother came to her apartment. 'My dear, are you very excited?'

'I am. Every moment I've been expecting Papa to change his mind. However did you persuade him?'

'He believes you'll be married before long and might not have the opportunity to travel again. He loves you, Victoria – as I do – and wants you to be happy.'

'Then why does he insist that I marry a rajah like him and not a Christian?'

Her mother smiled and reached over to stroke her face. 'Have you learnt so little about his faith, my love? To him all paths are the same – everyone, whether it be Christian or Hindu, are led to the Omnipresent One. He can't see why you're so anxious about it. You'll be able to continue to worship as you wish; perhaps you should settle for an Indian husband after all?'

Victoria shook her head. 'We've prayed that I might meet a suitable Englishman on one of these trips with Papa. I know it's unlikely, but there could be someone at the hotel in Delhi who would do. You've told me so much about England that I long to live there. Life would be so much more exciting away from all this ceremony. Please don't change your mind.'

'No, dearest; if marrying an Englishman is what you want, then I shan't stand in your way. I won't see you tomorrow morning; you'll be leaving too early. I shall say my farewells tonight.' They embraced and something soft slipped into Victoria's hand. 'A little spending money, my dear. I know how much you always buy at the bazaar in Bombay.'

She unclenched her fingers to find a small cloth purse stuffed full of rupees. Victoria tucked it into her crocodile handbag, hoping there would be an opportunity to sample the delights of shopping in Delhi.

* * *

Victoria was dressed and ready to leave long before the car pulled up under the portico to collect them. She and her father arrived at Victoria Terminus in good time for the train. She picked her way through the recumbent families, which were settled like nesting birds on the platform, surrounded by their belongings bundled in cotton squares. She was aware, as never before, of the gulf between her life and that of these people.

Aziz, her father's factotum, was waiting for them and ushered them into their carriage. She was a little apprehensive as this was the first time she had travelled in the family's private compartment and it meant being alone with Papa, without her ayah or her mother, for more than twenty-four hours.

The carriage was lined with dark brown mahogany and blue-black leather. She was amazed to discover they had their own shower and lavatory. The windows had heavy screens fitted outside, and solid external shutters so privacy was guaranteed, but if she couldn't even look out of the window the journey might well be tedious.

The train stopped occasionally at grand stations or wayside halts. Outside there were always teeming, noisy, chattering crowds and the calls of those selling nuts, sweets, fruits and drinks added to the cacophony. The shouts of 'Hindu pani' and 'Mussulman pani' from the water vendors catering for both religious persuasions made her wonder what Christians were to buy, and everywhere the tea sellers were shouting, trying to drown out the rest. Aziz fetched what he thought his 'family' needed and she was not allowed more than a glimpse of the platform.

The novelty had begun to pall, and the rattling of the train gradually lulled her into a fitful sleep as she stretched out comfortably on one of the leather-covered daybeds. She was jerked awake by the sound of screeching brakes as the train shuddered to a halt. There was the sound of shouting outside. Then her father was in front of her, standing shoulder to shoulder with his factotum, guarding her, whilst she was still struggling to sit upright.

The door of the carriage crashed open and a fair-haired English army officer filled the space. Her father was so outraged she almost laughed. He ordered the young soldier to remove himself at once, using his most perfect, formal English, every inch the wealthy Rajput gentleman.

The young man remained, politely waiting for

Papa to run out of invectives. When finally the soldier had space to speak, he half-bowed, totally ignoring her. She was hidden behind her protectors, but eager to discover exactly why they were now stationary at a deserted halt.

'I apologise for my intrusion, Rajah Sahib. Captain Henry Hindley-Jones at your service. The line ahead has been blocked and we're anticipating an attack by dacoits at any moment.'

Victoria shivered. She had heard about the bandits who held up trains and sometimes killed the travellers. Her father spoke rapidly in Hindi to Aziz, telling him to get the rifles, then bowed to the officer.

'Please excuse my outburst, Captain Hindley-Jones. My man and I will be out to join you immediately.'

The captain clicked his heels. 'Thank you, Rajah Sahib. Your help would be appreciated. My men are well trained, but we're going to need every gun we can get when they attack.'

She heard Aziz returning with the guns. He handed one to her father who tucked it expertly under his arm.

'We shall remain inside our entrance. I have no wish to leave my daughter unprotected. We both know how to use these.' He didn't suggest she join them outside, even though she could shoot as well as Aziz.

'Excellent! I suggest you secure the shutters.' The captain finally acknowledged her presence. 'You'll be quite safe, my lady.'

If the circumstances had been different she would have smiled at her elevation to the English aristocracy. Reluctantly her father stepped aside and she moved forward to offer her hand. Captain Hindley-Jones clasped it. His grip was firm, his hand calloused like a field worker's. A discreet cough from her father was enough to remind Victoria of her position. Although this man was English, and an officer, she was the only child of a wealthy and respected Brahmin and must consider herself his superior. She nodded, removing her hand.

'Please excuse me, Rajah Sahib, but I must return to my duties.' He clicked his heels again and backed out of the carriage. No one seemed to be frightened – the initial shouting had stopped. The only sound was of orders being issued by an Indian sergeant and the heavy bangs of doors and shutters being closed up and down the train.

Her father, with no sense of urgency, pointed to

the bathroom. 'Victoria, I suggest you take refuge in there. Aziz can place cushions and blankets on the floor. It will be quite safe. Lock the door and don't come out until I give you leave.'

'Shall I take a drink and some fruit as well?'

'If you want, but be quick; the attack could start at any moment.'

Without waiting to check that she obeyed his orders, he vanished outside to assist Aziz in fastening the shutters. With the same lack of haste her parent had displayed, she sauntered over to the fruit bowl and began to make her selection. There was the sound of raised voices outside as other travellers demanded to know what was going on. The clatter of boots racing past the compartment indicated the captain was marshalling his men ready to repel the bandits. She wondered how his troop of mounted men had happened to be in this remote place at exactly the right time. Divine intervention perhaps?

Smiling, she gathered up some fruit, a drink and a couple of books and prepared to retreat to the relative safety of the restroom. At least this ambush was a break in the tedium of the journey. Then the air was rent by the ugly sound of gunfire and a bullet tore through an unshuttered window, shattering the glass and spraying her with shards. For a moment she remained immobile – frozen with horror – then her father threw himself into the compartment and bundled her into the bathroom.

'Are you hurt, child? Here let me see your face.' He prised her fingers from her cheek. There was blood running down her face, but no pain. 'Nothing to worry about – superficial – wash it and put on a plaster.'

The door swung shut and she was alone, listening to the nightmare unfolding outside. Like an automaton she found a cloth and cleaned her face, but the blood kept coming. What should she do? She'd never had such a bad wound before and her head was beginning to swim. Was she going to bleed to death whilst the battle raged outside?

How could Papa not have realised she needed medical attention? She scrabbled about for a towel and pressed it hard to her cheek. Then when she turned to search for the medical box she caught a glimpse of her reflection in the mirror. This ashen-faced, bloodstained girl couldn't be her. She needed help. Panic-stricken, she forgot her instructions and fell out of the bathroom.

The rapid staccato of gunfire, the screams of women and children, the urgent shouts from the men drowned out her feeble cries for help. She stood, holding the towel to her face, oblivious to the bullets thudding into the unprotected side of the compartment. A second missile slammed into the carriage wall, covering her with splinters. She screamed, her voice echoing around the carriage. This time she was heard.

The English captain burst, for the second time that afternoon, through the door. 'For God's sake, get down. Now.'

Bewildered she looked at the carpet but didn't move. Two arms encircled her and flung her to the floor.

A third storm of bullets smashed through the broken window and several embedded themselves in a leather document case. She watched, squashed breathless by the weight of the soldier, as the bag leaped from the table as if possessed by a demon and flew across the room to thud heavily into the wall.

Her fall had dislodged the hand holding the towel and the sticky wetness was seeping out of the gash. Her hands were stinging from the splinters. She wanted this horror to stop. Wanted things to return to normal. Wanted to be back home. Tears dripped into the gory mess on her face.

She never cried – it wasn't done – but somehow,

however hard she tried to suppress them, her sobs escaped.

'Bloody hell! Don't cry, miss. It'll be all right. I'll keep you safe. Your father has already killed two of the bastards... sorry, beggars. We'll have them on the run soon.'

He rolled away, and held her against his chest as she shivered and cried. He raised his hand to smooth her hair and it came away red.

'Christ! You're hurt – I didn't realise. Sit up, sweetheart, let me have a look.'

She allowed him to push her up until she was supported by a table leg. For some reason she was no longer afraid. Her tears stopped and she faced her rescuer with absolute trust. His long, capable fingers examined the wound.

'You've lost a lot of blood and you're going to need stitches in this, but it's not nearly as bad as it looks.' He grinned, his teeth white. 'Can you reach that towel over there? We need to put it on your cut again.'

She nodded and bent her head in order to reach the cloth. To her consternation she toppled forward and a strange whirling blackness engulfed her. She came to, stretched out, as she had been at the start of the drama, on the daybed. But this time she was surrounded by a circle of anxious men.

Her father, his face twisted with anxiety, knelt at her side. 'Tory, my dear girl, I am so sorry. I should never have left you. Thank God Captain Hindley-Jones was here to assist you.'

At the mention of her rescuer's name her eyes searched the faces, but he wasn't there. Had he been curtly dismissed as an interloper as soon as her father had returned? So who were these men? Her face stung unpleasantly and she raised her fingers to investigate.

'No, please not to disturb the dressing, missy. I have placed several neat and helpful stitches in your injury.' The man who had spoken was obviously a doctor. He was dressed in white jacket, loose trousers and wore a white hat on his oiled-back hair, but his medical bag, on the floor beside him, looked reassuringly English.

'Where's the captain who saved me? I wish to thank him personally, Papa.'

'He has gone about his duties, child. There are prisoners to stow in the guard's carriage and order to restore outside. I'm certain he will be back to check that you're fully recovered as soon as he's free to do so.'

With that she had to be content. Aziz, who had been one of the men watching, moved back presumably satisfied that his master's most precious daughter was in no danger. She noticed that another man, obviously the doctor's assistant, was holding a basin, his brown face inscrutable, his white turban immaculate. Did she still require first aid?

'The doctor has to remove the splinters from your hands, my dear. Do you feel up to it?'

She nodded and instantly regretted it. 'Yes. I'm a little dizzy, but quite well enough to have my hands attended to.'

Although her eyes were averted she felt the doctor expertly removing the slivers. She gazed at Aziz, who was tidying the compartment, as though bullet damage and broken glass were part of his normal duties. His calmness did much to restore her calm.

'There, missy, all done now. You will have no scars on your hands.'

'Thank you, Doctor. I'm grateful for your assistance.'

The man salaamed and, talking rapidly in Hindi to his assistant, he vanished. He hadn't said that her face would be unmarked and she prayed this was an oversight. The noise of men's boots and raised voices continued outside for a while longer. Her father was no longer in the carriage. She was sure he was nearby but didn't feel ready to get up and investigate.

The shouting and stamping eventually stopped and the train was secure again and about to leave. Why hadn't her rescuer come back to enquire about her injuries? Then she heard the voice she had been waiting for: Captain Hindley-Jones was returning to see her.

She wished she had the energy to check her appearance before he came in; she must look grotesque with stiff white dressings on both hands and her right cheek. She tensed as footsteps approached the carriage. She recognised her father's voice, but could not distinguish what he was saying. She had no time to ponder as Aziz glided to the door and opened it smoothly.

The Englishman was ushered in ahead of her father and her face coloured. Giving the captain precedence was a sure sign he was in favour. Raising her head she stared, seeing him clearly for the first time. His eyes were so blue, like the sky first thing in the morning. Her tongue was too big for her mouth; her words of greeting remained locked behind her teeth.

He came over, his back parade-ground stiff, his manner formal.

'Miss Bahani, I'm pleased to see you sitting up and looking so much better. I'm sorry I had to leave so abruptly, but duty called.' His voice was deep, and far too loud for the small space of the carriage.

'I must thank you for saving my life, Captain. And I must apologise for losing control. I know that if I had listened to my father I would have been in no danger.'

Captain Hindley-Jones smiled and her skin prickled under the intensity of his gaze. 'I'm delighted to have been on hand when you needed me.'

She believed he would have said more but her father intervened. 'Captain, my daughter is tired and needs time to recuperate. I shall, of course, contact your commanding officer in Bombay to convey my thanks.'

The captain had no choice; he was dismissed. He bowed to her father and turned, treating her to another of his flashing smiles. Then he was gone, leaving her with more than dacoits to think about.

Twenty minutes later the train was rattling on its way to Delhi. It was almost dark and she hoped they would be stopping soon for supper. Papa had told her, when she'd asked if there was likely to be any further trouble, that the captain and some of his men, were accompanying the prisoners to make sure they remained safe from the remainder of the band. These men had evaded capture and galloped off into the desert.

Her mouth curved as she thought about the man who had rescued her so bravely; would his presence on the train mean she might have another opportunity to talk to him? She couldn't get him out of her mind.

'Papa, how did the captain and his troop come to be in the very place the dacoits planned to attack us?'

He smiled. 'It's his job to patrol this part of the railway line; look out for ambushes and chase away the bandits. Captain Hindley-Jones explained to me that he had been following this particular group. He had spotted their trail a day or so ago. An excellent young man. A credit to the Indian Army.' He frowned. 'However, I don't approve of the British being in positions of authority in *our* army. We have many first-rate young men of our own.'

'But you approve of *this* Englishman?'

'You must not worry, my dear. I'm not so ill mannered as to reveal my political opinions to this particular officer. He's an exception to my rule. I owe him everything.'

She would have to leave it there. Further discussion on the merits of the captain might reveal her interest in him. Could this be the opportunity her mother and she had envisaged? A chance encounter on the train with a suitable man?

She had an hour to make her decision. From the moment she had first seen him and their hands had touched, she had been drawn to him. He had saved her life – this made him a hero. He was English, a strong point in his favour. She closed her eyes, allowing her mind to recapture his image. He was far taller than Papa, which made him over six feet and his hair was the colour of ripe corn. She sighed – he had the most fascinating blue eyes she had ever seen.

Her hands throbbed and her face ached but she ignored them. Her head was whirling with the possibilities thrown in her way. However, it was against all her natural instincts to take the first step and she was certain he would not do so; he would lose his position if he did and she complained.

She had been raised with the expectation that her marriage would be arranged by her parents; now she was contemplating initiating a liaison with a complete stranger. She would be violating every rule, every tradition she had grown up with. It was the duty of a daughter and a wife to respect and obey the man of the household. What she was going to do was so bad her stomach roiled and her appetite vanished. Whatever the difficulties, she was going to make contact with the man that kismet had thrown in her path.

man of the household. What she was going to do was so bad her stomach rolled and her appetite vanished. Whatever the difficulties, she was going to make contact with the man that dinner had thrown in her path.

2

VISIT TO DELHI

Shortly before the train slowed for its scheduled supper stop, Victoria decided somehow to get outside the suffocating confines of the compartment. Whether she would have an opportunity to speak to the captain was in the lap of the gods. She was going to ask her father if she could stand on the platform whilst their servant bought the food. At first he was reluctant.

'Papa, it's so hot inside – could I please stand on the steps whilst Aziz fetches our supper? I'm feeling much better and my head doesn't hurt and neither do my hands.'

'It might be dangerous. Your mother would never forgive me if anything else happened to you.' His austere features softened a little. 'I rather think one incident a day is sufficient, my dear.'

'But there are soldiers on the train to guard the prisoners. I shall be perfectly safe just outside the door where you can see me.'

'Oh, very well, but don't leave the steps. Is that quite clear?'

'Of course I won't. Thank you. I've seen almost nothing so far. I'm supposed to be learning about my wonderful country – but I can hardly do that cooped up in here all the time, can I?'

He stared thoughtfully at her, as if seeing her for the first time. 'I do believe you have grown up and I hadn't noticed, my dear. I suppose I have to accept that you're an adult and I must let you have room to stretch your wings.' Aziz was summoned and instructed to fetch a soldier to stand with her.

She waited impatiently by the door, her heart thudding heavily, shivers of anticipation adding to her confusion. She had changed into an emerald green sari with gold edging, glad this traditional dress had no buttons or zips to struggle with. Brushing her hair had been painful and in the end she had abandoned the attempt and restrained it in a ribbon at the base of her neck.

Aziz appeared at the door, his lined face inscrutable under his turban, and announced the soldier was waiting outside. She stepped out expecting it to be black, for the shutters had been closed since the last stop and it was dark, but the many cooking fires and torches from the hundreds of food and drink vendors lit the platform like day.

She hardly dared look to see who was to guard her. She had decided, if it was Captain Henry Hindley-Jones, she would take this as a sign to grasp the opportunity and speak to him. She intended to explain who she was and give him her home address. She didn't care that she was behaving in a way both her parents would disapprove of.

She would not let this man vanish from her life – she might never have such a chance again. She would have liked to tell him she was not promised in marriage to anyone, that her mother was English and wished her to marry a fellow countryman and return to the land she still referred to as her home. She thought this information could wait until they were better acquainted.

She hoped her first name, and pale skin, would be enough to indicate her background. Mixed marriages were unusual and generally frowned upon by the rajahs and colonials alike, but such was her father's wealth and importance, and her mother's insignificance socially (she had been a governess to an English family) their union had gone mostly unremarked. Apart from her dark hair (not quite black like her father's) dressed in European fashions she was certain she could pass for British.

When she turned her head it was to see Captain Hindley-Jones standing stiffly correct beside her. He bowed and greeted her by name; she inclined her head slightly in response, but didn't answer. Aziz, satisfied they were not breaking any rules, hurried off to make his selections for their supper. As soon as the factotum turned his back the captain's face transformed. His eyes gleamed and his mouth curved.

'Good evening. I must say you look much better now, Miss Bahani.'

She smiled. His expression was telling her something far more exciting. 'If you remain where you are it will be quite permissible for us to converse, Captain Hindley-Jones. I have so much I want to tell you.'

He nodded. 'I prayed you would be allowed to come out when we stopped. It's the sole reason I'm on this train. I could have sent my sergeant.'

It took all her willpower to remain impassive – to not move closer and grasp his hand. 'We don't have much time. Could you tell me your address? I'm sure my mother will wish to write and thank you for your bravery.'

'I have a bungalow in the European enclave. Just a minute, I've a pencil somewhere; I'll write it down for you. But I warn you, I'm not there much – I'm away on patrol most of the time.'

He must guess it was she who wished to write to him. Aziz was returning. There wasn't much time. Frantically the captain scribbled the information and, under the very nose of her guardian, he bowed and slipped the scrap of paper into her injured hand. Then he bounded back down the metal steps to his position in the guard's van.

She dragged her gaze away to look at a group of women, chattering musically, as they pointed to the food they wanted for their families who were waiting hungrily on the train. The earlier encounter with the bandits did not seem to have dimmed anyone's appetite. Other people's food was normally served on wide, green banana leaves, but theirs was safely stored in woven boxes. Aziz waited for her to climb the stairs ahead of him, and without a further glance, she left the noisy platform and returned to the quiet of the private carriage.

She firmly pushed the idea that Captain Hindley-Jones might feel differently about their meeting out of her mind. She could almost hear her mother's voice warning her he might read any letter sent with amusement, and then toss it aside. She was certain he returned her interest. Eyes don't lie. All she had to do was steal the time, whilst in Delhi, to write him a letter. The money in her bag would be more than enough to pay for the postage. Mail could be handed in at a hotel reception desk and they would do the rest.

Two days after her arrival the hotel physician removed the cumbersome bandages and replaced them with small dressings. After this she was free to shop and visit freely, always accompanied by Aziz. It had taken all her ingenuity to deliver the letter to the concierge. As soon as this was done she was able to relax and enjoy her unaccustomed freedom. Henry was constantly in her thoughts – he was no longer Captain Hindley-Jones in her heart – and the trip dragged interminably. She was impatient to return and discover if he had replied to her.

* * *

Victoria arrived home nearly three weeks later in the full glare of the afternoon sun. The buildings shimmered and rolled under the haze as if no cloud had ever darkened the sky and no rain ever touched the earth. She supposed the baggage and her father's boxes of papers were unloaded, but it was no responsibility of hers. As long as her purchases were removed she would be content. The train remained stationary until this was completed, the time being taken up by a ceremonial greeting from the station-master before he escorted them to the waiting car.

Her sari stuck to her body; she almost expected it to give off heat when it touched the glowing upholstery. They drove into the flat, red landscape along the familiar road marked by groves of dark trees and clicking bamboos. The dust rose behind like an ominous cloud as if cutting off any hope of seeing Henry again.

She felt elated, and despondent, in equal measures, and in no mood to greet a house full of visiting relatives. Victoria knew her grandmother would have arrived in her absence, bringing uncles, aunts and sundry cousins, some of which were so distant the connection was invisible. At least two of these would be hoping to entice her into a declaration of devotion.

The landscape contained few points of interest. It took half an hour to drive along the private road to reach the high iron gates. The car passed into the drive that wound its way through dried-up parkland, over which truly beautiful trees were scattered.

However often she returned, this first glimpse of her home always thrilled her. The building stood, white and massive, among shady trees; it loomed through the waves of heat like a great liner at anchor. The car swept round a dramatic curve and entered the covered portico that projected from the front of building and then it drew to a halt before the short flight of wide marble steps. The palace had been built when elephants were still the mode of transport.

As expected she could see behind the tall windows that the interior was dark with people who were all eager to discover if she had enjoyed her brief venture into the outside world. They would all know about the dacoit attack and be straining to see if her injuries had left her scarred. They hadn't – for whoever the Indian doctor had been – he had known his business. All she had to show for her adventure was a faint pink line running from her ear to her brow, but she was able to hide this easily under her hair.

Regular trips to Bombay did not count; Delhi was the city everyone wanted to visit. If only they knew how much had changed since she had left, and it hadn't been Delhi that had altered her. Her lovely home was no longer enough; she could think of nothing else but her brief encounter. She believed she might have met the man she wanted to marry. She had written a long letter telling him all about her home, her family and her desire to visit England. She was certain his reply would be waiting for her.

After greeting her grandmother she pleaded exhaustion and hastily retired to her apartment for a cool shower and some much-needed privacy. Much as she loved her father, being cooped up with him for the two days of the return journey had been a strain. On the outside she had appeared to be his well-behaved only child, whilst inside she was bubbling with an excitement she daren't display. There was a soft swish as her bedroom door opened.

'Victoria, my darling, I've been so worried about you. What a dreadful experience. I must have made the journey dozens of times and we never saw so much as sniff of any bandits.' Her mother came across and sat beside her on the bed. 'Here, darling, let me see your poor face.' She tilted Victoria's head towards the light. 'I can hardly see the scar. It would have been such a pity if your face had been permanently marked.'

'Mama, there's so much I have to tell you. Did Papa mention how the English captain saved me?'

'He did, my dear. And I thank God he was there when you needed him.' She paused, a strange expression on her face. 'Was he a handsome gentleman by any chance?'

Heat flooded Victoria's face. 'Captain Hindley-Jones is the most wonderful, handsome man you could ever see. He must be over six feet tall and he was so strong, Mama; he picked me up as though I weighed no more than a feather.'

'Did you write and thank him for his assistance, by any chance?'

'He has replied? Oh, please, may I have it?'

Her mother delved into one of the deep pockets in her skirt and removed an unopened letter. 'I should really read this before I hand it to you, but I can see how much this means to you and so you may have it first. But when you have read it I must do so too.'

Victoria didn't care who read it as long as she was the first. Henry would not break any rules. Ignoring her mother, who was watching her closely, she tore the envelope open.

Dear Miss Bahani,
   I was delighted to receive your long letter. What an interesting family you have. I can

hardly imagine what it must be like living as you do surrounded by so much luxury.

My home in England, The Rookery, is small by comparison, but is considered large in the circle in which I move. It is set in a pretty park of around thirty acres. We also own several other smaller properties and farms in the vicinity.

My father, as a landowner, spends his days running the estate and managing his invest-ments. I believe we are considered well off and certainly my family is able to live comfortably. I am an only child and when I leave the army I shall assume responsibility for the estate.

My grandfather served in India which is why I am here today. His stories filled my head with exotic images and as soon as I left university I enlisted and here I am, a captain in the very same brigade as my grandfather.

If you have the time I would appreciate hearing how you have recovered. All corre-spondence breaks the monotony and is very welcome.

I remain yours sincerely,
Henry Hindley-Jones

He had told her everything she needed to know. He was wealthy, an only child and single. He had obviously realised the letter would be read by her parents and the information was as much for them as for her. Silently she handed the letter to her mother, watching her face closely as she read it.

'Well, Victoria, your Captain Hindley-Jones appears to be exactly the kind of man we hoped you'd meet. But it's too soon for you to decide if he's the one you wish to spend the rest of your life with. You spoke with him only a handful of times and in those extreme circumstances, anyone would have seemed attractive. I give you my permission to correspond with him, but I think it would be wise if we didn't mention this to your father.' She folded the letter and with a sweet smile handed it back. 'Now, are you coming down to join us? There are two young men Grandmother has brought especially to meet you.'

'I'd rather not, Mama. Could you excuse me for tonight? I really cannot find the energy to be polite to suitors that I have no intention of marrying. Meeting Henry was no accident. I truly believe he's the answer to my prayers. If he feels the same way I hope you will support his suit.'

Her mother's face creased with concern. 'My dear, things are changing so rapidly. You're not the girl who left here three weeks ago, but neither is your father the same man. Something has altered his mind about the role of the British here. I don't believe he will ever give his consent to you marrying an Englishman.'

'But you will still support me, won't you? Papa always listens to you. I'm sure between us we can persuade him.' She refused to be dispirited; after all, her father denied her nothing. If she truly wanted Henry he would not stand in her way.

After her mother left she wrote her reply. She told him about the pressure she was under to marry within her caste and explained how stifled she felt, constantly watched by family and servants who were all ready to carry a tale. Her ayah took the letter into Bombay to post.

With each letter she received her affection deepened until she believed she knew him well enough to invite him to come to Marpur. She didn't tell him she loved him, but hoped he had read between the lines, guessed how she felt. When he told her he was to attend a function in Bombay she was beside herself, for this was an event to which her entire family had been invited.

She discovered her mother in the garden attending to the roses. 'My dear, I wish you could see these flowers blooming as they should. They do not do well in our climate, however much attention they are given.'

'Mama, are we still attending the reception on Friday?'

'Yes, have you changed your mind? Do you wish to stay at home?'

'No, I'm looking forward to it.' Should she mention Henry was going to be there? 'I wish I could introduce you to Captain Hindley-Jones. Do you think I could invite him here sometime?'

Her mother looked up from her pruning with a slight frown. 'Good heavens, are you still corresponding with that gentleman?'

'You know I am. Didn't I tell you the other day that I love him?'

'Darling girl, you cannot possibly be in love with a gentleman you've only met the once. It is no more than infatuation; when you see him I'm certain you will realise you have built him into something he is not.'

'We have been exchanging letters these past weeks. I know him; he's no longer a stranger to me – whatever you might think. I think I shall not go on Friday after all. Such occasions bore me.'

Her mother's smile incensed her, but she forced

back her anger. It would not do to upset her, as it was imperative she be allowed to attend the reception.

'No, Victoria, you will attend as planned. Mixing with your own kind will soon put him from your mind. I should never have allowed you to correspond with him so freely; this is my fault. He is not the romantic hero you have turned him into.'

'What is he, Mama?'

'An ordinary English gentleman, quite unsuitable for someone like you. Your father has decided you should marry one of your distant cousins. There are a dozen or more to choose from.'

Horrified, Victoria shook her head. 'I've no wish to be married to anyone. I'm not even eighteen. Do you wish to be rid of me so soon?'

'Of course not, my love, there's no hurry at all. Let us forget all about the subject and decide what you shall wear on Friday.'

* * *

Victoria was disappointed she could not wear the oyster silk evening dress she had bought in Delhi. Mama was most insistent that their European clothes should be abandoned. In future she must always appear in traditional dress. Her closet shelves were piled high with a kaleidoscope of saris, and tonight she chose an amber silk with bands of real gold thread embroidery.

'Victoria, my love, that's an excellent choice. Elegant and expensive, exactly the impression I wish you to give tonight. The topaz stones woven through your hair are the perfect finishing touch.'

'I almost didn't recognise you, Mama; it's so rare you wear a sari. Is Papa not coming with us?'

'No, my dear, he's been called away to a business meeting of some sort. He hopes to join us later.'

The car was waiting outside under the portico, the headlights attracting myriads of moths, the noise from the undergrowth almost deafening. For some reason the flickering flambeaux did not have the same effect on the night creatures.

Aziz salaamed and slammed the car door shut. Tonight they were to be free from his too-observant eyes. Victoria thanked God she would be able to find Henry without it being reported to her father. She settled back in the darkness, relieved her mother did not wish to make conversation. The silence gave her time to rehearse what she would say when she eventually came face to face with the man she was determined to marry.

'My dear, you're very quiet tonight. Are you unwell?'

'I was enjoying the peace. It will be so noisy at the party and I do have a slight headache.' She hesitated, hating to lie to her mother. 'Will it be acceptable for me to leave the reception and walk about in the garden if it becomes too much.'

'Of course you may, Victoria. But if you feel you wish to return, send a servant to fetch me.'

The car joined a line of similar vehicles. In the few minutes it took to reach the entrance Victoria gazed at the guests who alighted. For the first time there were few white faces amongst the brown. Did this mean Henry would no longer be attending?

Inside the noise and heat were almost unbearable. The press of people in the vast marble entrance hall made progress all but impossible. Her mother clasped her elbow.

'Victoria, if we should get separated make your way to the terrace. I had no idea there would be so many invited. I'm not surprised your papa discovered he had an urgent meeting elsewhere.'

'Do we have to stay? I'm sure with so many hundreds here we will not be missed.'

'I have dismissed the chauffeur. It will take an hour at least for him to be fetched back. Smile, my love, we must look as though we are enjoying being crushed like sardines in a can.'

They were swirled along by the crowd until they reached the ballroom. Here it was possible to detach oneself and find a space to breathe more freely. 'Mama, your friends are beckoning. Please go and join them; I shall escape onto the terrace.'

'Come and find me when you are ready to leave. If we remain until ten o'clock, supper is served then and that is always worth waiting for.' She laughed. 'Your father is arriving then. Do you think you can bear to stay so we can return together?'

'Of course I can. It will be no hardship to sit outside; it's just in here it's too oppressive.'

Outside the terrace was all but empty. She drifted across to the balustrade and leant against it, the cool stone beneath her fingers steadying her pulse. He was here, not as a guest as she'd supposed, but on duty guarding the perimeter with his men. He was in the garden. Although he'd not acknowledged her, he must have seen her. Standing as she was beneath the glare of the torches she would be clearly visible to anyone in the garden below.

She remained in full view for several minutes before retreating to the shadows at the far end of the terrace. Her knees were trembling; if she did not find a bench to sit on soon she would collapse.

She closed her eyes and allowed his image fill her head. Mama was wrong; he was every bit as wonderful as she'd remembered. He was a head taller than his troopers and even in the darkness his fair hair shone. How long would she have to huddle here before he came to find her?

Heavy footsteps approached. She shrunk against the wall. If it wasn't him, what would she do?

'Victoria, darling girl, I cannot believe you are here. Let me look at you.' Henry reached down and drew her to her feet. Her hands were lost in his. She gazed up, her heart hammering, unable to respond.

'Henry... I don't... I must...' She faltered, was silent, unable to speak for happiness.

'I cannot stay long, I'm on duty, but I'm coming to speak to your father as soon as I can get leave. Have you changed your mind? Do you want me to come?'

'Please, come as soon as you can. Things are changing; even my mother is against us. I fear my father will never agree to us being together.'

His fingers gripped hers. 'Sweetheart, don't despair. Somehow we will prevail; I will convince your father that I am the man for you.'

Loud voices at the far side of the terrace startled

them apart. 'You must go, Henry. We cannot be seen together. I shall be counting the days until you come to me.'

He gathered her closer, dropped a feather-light kiss on her lips and released her. Before she could say her goodbyes he had vanished into the darkness. Now all she had to do was wait patiently until he arrived at Marpur.

Several long, slow weeks dragged by with no sign of him. He was often away on patrol so Victoria tried to console herself with the thought that this was why he had not arrived. No further letters were exchanged; her mother had made sure of this. She began to fear she had imagined the connection, that her feelings were not reciprocated. She had met, and dismissed, two more hopeful young men, much to her grandmother's annoyance. She was reluctantly dragged into games of tennis, swimming parties and shopping trips to Bombay. Then everything changed.

Her father finally accepted that he could not parade suitors in front of her, allow her to attend adult parties, and still treat his daughter as a child when she was at home. In the Bahani family there were babies, children and adults. Each had a clearly defined place in the hierarchy. Babies were usually not seen at all and never after sundown. Children ate separately in the evening when there was company, and then retired to their rooms to read. It was within this second category she had been caged.

From tonight she should be joining in the set of rituals that until now she had only glimpsed from the veranda. She was to be included when adult family and visitors gathered at dusk, under the sweet-smelling limes on the lawn, for sundowners. She decided to wear her new tangerine silk sari in honour of the occasion. She was downstairs waiting when her father appeared in the hall.

'Are you ready, Victoria? From tonight everything will be different. You will have responsibilities and your opinion will be respected.'

'I am ready, Papa. If I'm old enough to be married, to accompany you to parties, then I'm more than ready to join you in the evenings.'

Her father led her across the lawn, the grass crisp underfoot, towards the long cane chairs arranged in a semi-circle – imposing ones in the middle, more modest at the extremities. He sat down on the most elaborate and she, just this once, sat down next to him, in what was normally her mother's place.

Victoria watched with interest as the others strolled out to join them. The men all wore high-necked, close-buttoned black coats, and white trousers cut like jodhpurs. The ladies, their freshly oiled hair glistening in the evening sunshine, glittered and swayed, like gossamer flowers, in their saris, moving in little hesitant bunches. When they did finally settle they were all on her left, while the men took up positions on her father's other side. Her mother had decided to wait with her grandmother, who never came out, in the drawing room.

Drinks were then served on silver trays in crystal glasses: whisky for the men and a mango cocktail for the ladies. As she was sipping her drink there was the unmistakable sound of a car approaching. Looking up she saw the headlights flickering in and out of the trees.

Conversation stopped. Everyone looked enquiringly at her father, but he was equally perplexed. She guessed who was coming at such an inauspicious moment. It had to be Henry, at last. It would be a disaster; everybody knew it was not correct to call so late. Her father and her relatives would not be impressed by this breach of protocol.

Fortunately it was almost dinner time and, as was the custom, ladies were drifting in to join those waiting in the comfort of the drawing room. Hastily she arose, and trying not to look as though she was hurrying, headed for the safety of the house.

* * *

God damn it! The bloody place was supposed to be barely five miles from Bombay. It hadn't seemed that way; the road twisted and turned like a snake, making driving in the pitch-dark hazardous and unpleasant. Henry was already regretting his decision to drive to Marpur Palace that evening and not wait until the following morning as he'd first intended.

As the wheel of his car dropped for the umpteenth time into a pothole, throwing him to one side and jerking the wheel from his hand, he swore again. He should have telephoned Victoria and told her he was coming. He thought it might be bad form to arrive unannounced after dark, but he only had twenty-four hours' leave, and he was desperate to see her again and to make their relationship official.

It was so bloody hot. Even with the windows down he was choking on the thickness of the evening air. Was he mad to come out here on the strength of a handful of letters and three brief meetings? His commanding officer would demote him instantly, might even throw him out of the army, if he ever discovered he was planning to marry a native.

He had read and reread the letters she had sent him; could recite them off by heart. He knew more about her, how she felt, what she thought, than anyone else alive, even his parents. His lips twitched as he thought of them, so staid and conventional in their freezing barracks of a house back home. God knows what they'd think of his involvement with a girl of mixed race, however exotic and aristocratic her background.

He was not given to impulses, was known throughout the regiment as a steady and reliable chap. But for some reason when he'd held her in his arms, heard the bullets thudding into the sides of the carriage, he'd known she was the woman for him. Meeting her again at the reception had confirmed his belief. She was far too young, not even eighteen, and he was going to ask her to leave her family to become an army wife. Was this expecting too much of her? In the current circumstances would her father give his consent?

Thank God! The gates – there was a long drive through the park but from now on it was flat. In the distance he could see the flickering lights of the massive palace. She said it looked like a liner and although he was not given to such flights of fancy, he was forced to agree.

His car bucketed and shuddered its way down the drive and, in the shimmering light of his headlamps, he could see there were people gathered on the lawn under the lanterns, most of them reclining on some sort of deckchair.

As he drove up the final stretch he was aware that every head was turned towards him. All were now on their feet and all were staring at him. The men were arranged like black crows on one side of the rajah, the women – a fluttering group of kingfishers – on the other. They didn't look at all friendly.

He switched the engine off. He could feel runnels of perspiration trickling down his back; his hands were clammy – good God, he'd faced battles with more equanimity. He got out of the car, surreptitiously pulling down his jacket, and tucked his shako under his arm. He was shaking, but the familiar contours of his hat gave him a modicum of confidence and it stopped his damn hands from trembling like a girl's.

The rajah was on his way to greet him. The men trailed behind, not speaking and definitely not smiling. Then he saw a servant, his white shirt tails flashing in the darkness, racing across the park to deliver some sort of verbal message to Victoria's formidable father.

He looked across to the veranda and saw a tall woman, obviously not Indian, with Victoria close beside her. Both were in native dress. The message had obviously come from this woman and it seemed to do the trick. No longer advancing like an outraged adjutant, the man he hoped would be his father-in-law was faintly smiling as he walked up to him, his hand extended.

'Good evening, Captain Hindley-Jones. This is an unexpected pleasure, but a pleasure nonetheless.'

3

HENRY'S ARRIVAL

Victoria's grandmother greeted her precipitous arrival with a reproving look, but Mama glanced up from her conversation with Romala, the wife of one of the many cousins, with a smile of welcome. She was always shocked to see her lovely English mother looking like a pale moth among so many vivid but-terflies.

Until recently she had rarely adopted the tradi-tional mode of dress and still favoured the plain style and muted colours she had worn as a governess. Only now, of course, they were made to fit from finest silk and cotton lawn. Her fading blonde hair was still worn in a soft chignon and it suited her delicate oval face to perfection.

When Victoria had asked her once how she had resisted her mother-in law's insistence she adapt to Bahani ways, her mother had told her she merely ignored the instructions. So like a stone upon which water dripped, she remained intrinsically herself, but happy to live in the way her husband wished. Things were different today and her mother was in traditional dress; however, her sari was coffee silk with a narrow gold edging.

Mama patted the soft cushioned seat of the Chesterfield. Victoria hastened across the acres of Afghan and Persian carpets, relieved that she did not have to walk over the black and white tiled floor on which her high-heeled sandals would have clipped noisily.

'What is it, my love? Tell me.'

Victoria was shivering as she shifted closer. Shaking her head dumbly, she stared at the wide open windows leading onto the veranda. 'It's Henry – he has come.'

Always astute, her mother followed her anguished gaze and saw the wavering headlights of the car, so close. The vehicle was almost in sight. 'Oh dear!'

There was no need to say anything more. Victoria waited for the deluge of disapproval to pour over her. Why hadn't Henry made enquiries before setting out? If only he'd thought to ask, she would have told him to delay and not come until tomorrow. Indeed, to ring first, to announce his impending visit.

She prayed to all the gods she knew that they would not be swept away; that having come at last to find her his visit would not be in vain. The sound of the car, a powerful one, was audible inside. Her father, and the uncles and cousins, would be on their feet, united in their opprobrium. Poor Henry, how would he cope with such a forbidding welcome? She felt sick and perspiration trickled, unladylike, between her shoulders.

Grandmother rapped her cane on the floor to get attention. 'There is a person arriving in a car. Is anyone expecting a visit at such a time as this?' The tone was icy, so scathing Victoria could not unlock her voice to answer.

'Yes, Mother-in-law, I believe it's Captain Henry Hindley-Jones. I was expecting him tomorrow, but obviously I've mistaken the day.' Her wonderful, brave mother rose majestically and, like a swan, sailed across the floor bringing Victoria along in her wake. They exited from the French windows and walked, no glided, down the veranda, towards the group of men and the fine car pulling up beside them.

Her heart was swooping and diving in turn. No girl ever had such a mother. Victoria watched her as she leant against the carved rail, raising her hand imperiously. Instantly a servant appeared at her feet and Mama spoke rapidly to him in Hindi and he ran off with the message.

The servant arrived just as Henry stepped from his car. Her feet left the floor – she was floating – awash with love. He was even more handsome, even more noble, even more commanding tonight.

His uncovered fair hair gleamed as the lantern light caught it. His shoulders were back, his spine ramrod stiff, but he held his shako under his arm in a death grip. Its stiffened sides were bending under the pressure. Surely her father would recognise him as the man who had saved his daughter from the bandits so bravely?

To her relief whatever message her mother had conveyed was sufficient. Papa stepped forward, salaamed, then offered his hand. Henry bowed, almost in half, and saluted before taking the hand. Her mother carefully prised her fingers from beneath hers, before sweeping round to vanquish the more deadly foe – Grandmother.

This ancient relative looked and acted like Queen Victoria in a sari. The best one could hope for was to be ignored, for Grandmother only became interested when anyone committed a major misdemeanour. Her gimlet eyes, black beads in a currant pudding, unerringly sought her granddaughter out. Had her pallor and nervousness given her away?

Her mother spoke first. 'Mother-in-law, you must excuse us; we have to greet our guest. It's the English captain who saved Victoria from the dacoits.'

'That's as may be. Has the man no manners to be arriving at this time? Why has he come, Daughter? Did you invite him to visit?'

A rustle of eager apprehension rippled round the waiting women. Like jackals they sensed a kill and gathered themselves, ever ready to pounce on the unfortunate victim.

'I did, Mother-in-law. I thought it appropriate to thank him in person. He's stationed in Bombay so I invited him to call in when next he had leave.'

Victoria and her mother left the seething gathering before Grandmother had time to reply. Papa's voice was clear and coming towards the portico. There was the crunch of booted feet on gravel. In spite of her fear her mouth curved. She should wait in a dignified and docile silence beside her mother.

The joy of seeing the man she had come to know so well, with whom she already had an understanding, overcame her natural caution.

It was incredible she had fallen in love with Henry after three brief meetings, but that was how things were. They were meant to be together and she intended to let *nothing* keep them apart. There was a restraining arm about her shoulders; her mother understood, even if she disapproved. Victoria didn't have to convince *her* of the sincerity of her feelings.

Her father appeared in the entrance flanked by a silent band of black-coated crows. The uncles and cousins enjoyed picking over the bones as much as the women. They were all invisible to her. She saw only Henry, his sky blue eyes glittering with emotion, his smile an invitation. He stood erect and alone in the doorway. Without her mother's hand she would have run forward and flung herself into his waiting arms.

In the endless silence of that moment she could hear the clock ticking, the cicadas clicking, her heart beating, and the growing hum of disapproval coming from behind.

Her mother smiled. 'Captain Hindley-Jones. I am so glad to meet you at last. You are very welcome.

Have you been obliged to ride far today before coming out to visit us?'

Henry cleared his throat. 'You're most gracious, Rani Sahib. I've just ridden in from the desert, a journey of twenty miles. Unfortunately the dacoits have rebanded and we must be even more vigilant.'

'Then I feel sure you must be tired after such a strenuous day and will wish to retire for the night. I shall have a tray sent to your room.'

Instantly aware he was *de trop* he bowed and thanked Mama politely, his voice so deep and powerful the words he spoke were irrelevant. Her mother made a small gesture, which sent servants scurrying to accomplish her wishes. A suite in the guest quarters would be ready quicker than he could be escorted there. So without being able to exchange a word directly, he vanished behind Aziz, down the long marble corridor that led to the rear of the property.

The harsh clang of the dinner gong temporarily prevented her grandmother's outburst. 'Mama, I feel unwell. May I retire?'

'Yes, my dear. Run along. It would be better not to be here when your father approaches and demands answers.'

Victoria fled upstairs. The hot stares of accusation scorched her back as her flight was tantamount to admitting guilt. She didn't care what anyone thought; even if she had to wait until she reached her majority, she would marry Henry.

Her ayah was waiting for her; here a word spread faster than action. She suffered her maid's ministrations and then she was, at last, in her cool cotton nightdress and the servant slipped away. A tray of fruit and sweet rolls, and a jug of iced water, stood on the table by the open French windows.

She was too wound up to sleep. Tonight the softly whirring, paraffin-powered overhead fan was a source of irritation. She could hear the insects immolating themselves on the fly screens, drawn to their death by her bedroom lights. Unable to bear the sound she went round the lamps and plunged the room into darkness. Immediately there was a constriction in her chest. She was suffocating – the hot, black darkness became a prison. She had to get into the coolness of the night.

The scent of jacaranda and orange blossom from the garden below was overpowering as she stepped onto the balcony, but she couldn't see the plants. This was impossible without standing on a chair. Privacy was paramount for, as always, it wouldn't do for anyone to be glimpsed in their dishabille, but at least she was part of the darkness.

The stars had never shone so brightly, nor the moon bathed her in such brilliance. Unexpectedly she heard the sound of footsteps on the gravel below. A quiver of excitement spiralled round her body. It could only be him; everyone else wore soft shoes or sandals.

Was he looking for her room? He must be. She flattened herself against the stone and called out softly, not daring to raise her voice. Grandmother's spies were always lurking somewhere, ready to report misbehaviour. The footsteps paused. No one spoke, but seconds later a missile flew over her high balcony wall and thudded heavily at her feet. As she stooped to recover the object she heard him disappear into the night.

Unwrapping the intricate parcel in moonlight was impossible so she carried the treasure back to her room. Hastily relighting a lamp, she retreated to the sanctuary of her bed. When she released the billowing whiteness of the mosquito net she was immediately cocooned inside. Here she could safely investigate this unexpected gift.

Her hands were shaking. She could scarcely untie the string that held the soft green material together.

Inside was a square, polished wooden box, about eight inches by five, inlaid with mother-of-pearl in a flower pattern. After carefully lifting the lid she found a second box, made this time from woven reeds and sealed with a single string of multicoloured glass beads. There would be another one inside; it was like the Russian doll her father had given her for her ninth birthday.

Slowly she unpeeled the layers until, inside the fifth, in a tiny cloth jewel bag, she discovered the treasure. A letter folded many times and a silver and ivory locket in the shape of a heart. This she put to one side whilst she smoothed out the paper. The words seemed to bounce off the page as if the writer had flung them there. The scrawl was achingly familiar.

Dearest Victoria,

I have treasured every letter you sent and have missed being able to exchange correspondence with you. I have reread them countless times My dearest Victoria, I must apologise for arriving so late and unannounced. I should have waited until tomorrow, but I could not bear another night without a glimpse of your lovely face. As soon as I was free from my duties I borrowed a car and set off. I only have a twenty-four-hour pass and it will be half over by tomorrow morning.

Seeing how you looked on my entrance has given me the courage to write what is in my heart. What I'd hoped to be able to say to you face to face. My darling girl, I have thought of you constantly since our brief meetings on the train. Then when we met again, I knew I was not mistaken in my feelings. I ask myself, how is it possible to know you are the one I have been waiting for all my life? I can't explain it, my dear, but I am certain we are meant to be together.

I have treasured each of your letters and on each reading my feelings grew stronger. It is going to be difficult, but whatever the outcome of tomorrow's meeting with your parents, please don't despair. Somehow we shall pre-vail and eventually be together as man and wife.

Your family is aristocratic, rich and influen-tial and I am merely a British Army officer. My background is respectable and although I am not wealthy at the moment, I have a reasonable income and will be able to keep you in an ac-

ceptable style. As the only child I shall inherit a considerable fortune eventually.

You mentioned several times in your letters how much you long to visit England – one day we shall be there together.

Sleep well, my dearest Victoria, and dream of me as I shall dream of you.

My love forever,

Henry

Oh, Henry! She held the letter to her heart, tears of happiness trickling down her cheeks. He returned her love. She had not been mistaken. Nothing mattered – she could endure whatever happened next now she knew that he loved her.

The images engraved on the locket were also of flowers and vines entwined, and the ivory petals shimmered in the lamplight. The tiny clasp released the halves revealing, in one, a miniature likeness of Henry. The other was empty, waiting for her to place her photo or similar memento. Shakily she fastened the delicate silver chain around her neck, vowing never to take it off again, not even to bathe.

She reread the letter many times before finally extinguishing the light. Much later she heard her parents walk past and then the house drifted into quiet. She scarcely slept, repeatedly falling asleep then jerking awake with racing heart and clammy skin.

* * *

At dawn she was bathed and dressed, ready to escape. At this time only the small army of invisible untouchables would be awake and completing their unpleasant tasks. If she could leave her rooms undetected she might somehow contrive to meet Henry and still be able to return before her ayah arrived with the breakfast tray.

In the near darkness she crept downstairs, like a wraith, in a pale lemon sari, her head covered to hide her hair. On soft feet she fled along the empty corridor and out into the garden. The grass was damp from its nightly watering and in moments her silk slippers were soaked and her sari clung to her ankles. She hugged the perimeter of the building, under the veranda, for there she would be invisible to prying eyes. She hurried towards the rear of the house where the guests' suites were situated.

She had to see him, have one meeting free from constraints, before he faced her parents. It was barely light; she had an hour until her disappearance would be discovered. How this meeting was to be accomplished she had no idea, but if the gods were with her she would discover him. She hesitated at the corner, listening for the sound of busy servants. Her unexpected appearance would be noted and the information relayed instantly to her father, or worse, to her grandmother.

Her feet were cold and wet, she shivered constantly and for a moment regretted her decision and wished she had stayed in her room. The thought of her father's anger if he found out increased her shaking. She was insane; she must go back immediately before anyone saw her.

Too late – someone was coming. She remained hidden, poised between fear and hope, and waited for the person to materialise. Her beloved strode around the corner, head down, deep in thought. He might have passed her by if she hadn't moved instinctively towards him. He stopped, astonished. His eyes met hers and then the hard planes of his face dissolved in delight.

'Victoria, my angel, come to me.' He opened his arms and she stepped in. As he gathered her close she relaxed. Now she had nothing to fear; she was safe. She was home. Slowly his embrace warmed her and she stopped shivering. She inhaled his smell –

lemon soap and tobacco – and imprinted it on her memory. Her cheek was resting on the roughness of his khaki jacket, her hands flat against his chest, but the buckle from his belt was pressing into her and she pulled back a little.

Tilting her face she gazed at him. 'Henry! I'm so pleased to see you. Why has it taken you so long to come? I was beginning to think you'd changed your mind and no longer felt the same.'

His arms tightened and her feet left the ground as he twirled her around. 'Darling girl, how could you doubt me? I told you that I loved you at the reception. I meant every word I said in my letter. I intend to marry you – however long it takes. In fact I'm going to make you a vow. Whatever the obstacles on my side or yours, we shall prevail. You're the future Mrs Henry Hindley-Jones.'

As she slid down his heated body, a strange electricity rippled through her. She became hot from toes to crown. 'It's going to be difficult. My mother no longer supports our cause. Things are changing politically and being seen to be pro-British is not acceptable to my father.'

'Whatever happens, my darling, you must be strong and wait for me. I shall overcome every argument, but it might take time.'

4

SEPARATED FOREVER

Victoria rested, content, in the warmth of his arms under the veranda. She knew, whatever she wanted, their relationship was doomed. The election of Subhas Chandra Bose as president of the Indian National Congress earlier that year meant feeling against the British, and soldiers in particular, was running high.

Her father no longer wore European clothes and foreign goods were boycotted in the household. Although he had supported Gandhi's non-violent protest in his youth he, like many of his friends, was moving towards a more aggressive stance to gain independence. He was quite definitely no longer pro-British. In such an atmosphere, how could a union between them be considered? The only hope of being together was to wait until she reached her majority, but four years was a long time and the political situation was uncertain. By the time she was twenty-one it was unlikely the Indian Army would still have British officers. It was possible she might never see him again.

'Don't cry, sweetheart. However long it takes we will be united eventually.'

'I cannot bear to wait four years. You could be recalled to England and lost to me forever.'

'Things are not good in Europe. I fear there could be war. Talk in the officers' mess is of an early recall, but I promise I will not leave without you.'

She was about to protest when his mouth closed over hers. For a few blissful minutes her worries vanished. Her fingers locked behind his neck and she pressed against him. His tongue slid along her lips and waves of heat engulfed her. Too soon he raised his head leaving her wanting more.

'Enough, darling, I must not be found here with you – it might ruin everything.' His eyes glittered as he gently pushed her away. 'Go in. You're not dressed warmly enough. I love you, and I always keep my promises.'

The sun was almost above the horizon; their

short time together was over. If she was to return to her room unobserved she had to leave immediately. He shook his head, unable to speak. She could not say goodbye; reaching out, she pressed her fingers on his lips and turned to go.

He crushed her to him a second time before pushing her away. His cheeks were wet as he smiled a farewell. She slunk back along the wall, hiding her tears beneath her sari. He was the first man she had kissed, but if she could not be with him she vowed he would also be the last.

Somehow she must compose herself. She almost wished, at that moment, she had never met him. Life would be so much easier if she could return to being her old untroubled self, someone with nothing more exacting to do than attend parties and picnics with her friends, and reject, every few months, the suitors sent for her approval.

Becoming an adult was irreversible. She could never go back to being a carefree child again. Whatever the outcome of Henry's visit, grandmother's matrimonial plans were doomed to failure.

By the time her breakfast tray arrived she had changed back into her nightgown and hidden the wet clothes and ruined slippers. However hard she tried, she was unable to swallow more than a sip of juice.

She heard her parents pass her apartment and go downstairs earlier than was customary.

Twenty minutes later there was the sound of Henry's car as he drove away, taking her heart with him. Strangely she didn't blame them, didn't hate them for what they'd done. She would have done the same herself. How odd being an adult was! It would be social and business suicide for her father to allow his only daughter to marry a British soldier. She must never let her parents know how she really felt. They loved her; she was their only child. It would destroy them to know their actions were causing her such intolerable pain.

Downstairs her mother greeted her with her customary soft smile and kiss, and made room on the sofa. 'Good morning, darling. You look a little pale. Did you not sleep well?'

'It was too hot, but I shall have a rest this afternoon.' Victoria smiled with what she hoped was reassurance. 'I'm quite well, Mama – don't worry about me.'

The conversation returned to the topic of a proposed picnic and crocodile hunt without any sideways glances or raised eyebrows. She forced herself to relax and after a while was able to join in the plans with a show of enthusiasm. Her father and the uncles joined them and the talk turned to politics. In this house women were not excluded from such discussions. And so the day passed; her appetite did not return, but she was able to push the food around her plate sufficiently to disguise this.

Henry was not mentioned again, not even by her mother. It was going to be hard having no one to talk to about her heartache. Her mother understood what her hopes had been. It seemed incredible that the matter was never to be discussed. This must be her father's decision – her mother could never be so cruel.

She retired, only a little earlier than usual, feeling she had acquitted herself well. As she settled down, enshrouded in her white nest, she allowed her control to slip. Eventually drained, her pillow sodden, she tried unsuccessfully to sleep.

His visit might never have happened; to her family Henry didn't exist. Her parents and relatives had wiped him from their collective memories, leaving her alone in her misery. For the first time in her life she could not go to her mother for comfort.

Now all hope had gone and there was nothing to look forward to. She wished during the long, sleepless night she could remove him from her heart; not have to face a future where his absence would remain like a knife in her side every second of the day and night. She could not continue writing to him as any replies would be confiscated before they reached her.

* * *

The countless days crawled past and life, for everyone else, continued unchanged. One morning, three weeks after Henry's visit, she was sitting listlessly, listening to her family discussing a rumour that a pack of wild dogs was moving through the jungle and drifting nearer to them day by day.

'Game has been getting scarcer, even in our own jungle. Surely that's confirmation enough?'

'Indeed it is, Romala. Our servants and their families are beginning to go short of meat. Of course we can manage quite well on wild pigeon and jungle fowl, but I do miss having venison.'

Victoria looked at her mother. When had she become so interested in what she ate? She couldn't find the energy to ask and settled back in her chair to gaze unfocused at the assembled group. Vaguely she heard her father and the uncles decide they ought to organise a hunt. There had been an invitation to join another uncle and his family on a camping expedition for a day or two. This meant the two things could be achieved simultaneously.

'Victoria, my dear, you'd like to go away on a little holiday for a few days wouldn't you?'

'Yes, Mama, that would be nice.' She sat up feeling more animated than she had for weeks. The thought of escaping from her home appealed.

She heard her mother say everyone would go, apart from Grandmother, who would remain in residence alone. The camp was to be sited near a river that lay twenty miles or so across country, most of which consisted of thick, foothill jungle.

They were to leave early, well before dawn. If they travelled slowly, and quietly, her father hoped he could look into the rumours. They might not kill the wild dogs, but would almost certainly succeed in driving them away to other, easier hunting ground.

Her sleepless nights and lack of appetite were beginning to show. She had lost weight and her eyes were dark and shadowed. Although she continued to smile, she was finding it increasingly difficult to join in the general banter. However hard she tried to hide it, her parents must be aware she was desperately unhappy. She was sure this hastily arranged excursion was more to distract her, than to search for a rumoured dog pack.

* * *

They were travelling in more comfort than usual, using two bullock carts; the second was loaded with camping gear and personal luggage. She almost wished she was riding with the men, but inertia prevented her from speaking.

The jungle was rarely still, especially in the early morning and at evening time. As they voyaged she was aware of the presence of numberless spectators. Parrots and parakeets flickered overhead and monkeys displayed their amusement as they peeped through the heavy leaves with unimpressed eyes. A scrumple of sand across the track showed the slither marks of a snake's crossing.

'Look, Victoria, do you see the tiger's pug marks running across our path?' her mother asked.

She did see them, deeply indented, and in spite of knowing she had the protection of the many guns of the bearers and her father and uncles, she became inexplicably tense and anxious. She glimpsed, around a twist in the track, the tail end of the dog pack. The bullocks halted of their own volition, sweating and shivering. Her father had his rifle ready and managed to fire a single shot before the pack disappeared, leaving one of their number yelping in the dust.

'Good shot, sir. He's done for,' one of the uncles exclaimed, his voice loud in the silence following the report.

Her father rode up and, leaning from his saddle, prodded the carcass with the barrel of his rifle. 'Dead. Come and get it, Aziz.'

Victoria stared at the body – even in death it wore an ungracious look. Aziz slung it into his wagon and the little caravan moved off again. The quiet did not last long and soon there was the accompaniment of the usual chorus of yells, coughs and cackles and the familiar noises soothed her a little.

Uncle Sydney had chosen a beautiful site for his camp. It was at a place where the river shoaled, running green over white rounded boulders. The low cliffs, and the far bank, had at their shoulder the fringes of the real jungle where green and purple merged into the hills.

'Isn't this lovely, Victoria? Look how well your uncle has arranged things for us.'

She sat up and glanced around. Three marquees stood in the shade of a grove of cotton trees, though far enough from them to avoid the danger of snakes and other crawling things. They were cool and private. Smaller tents, for the servants, had been placed at a discreet distance; they were in the full glare of the sun. Aunt Kunthla, massive in an emerald sari, moved about distractedly organising the kitchen staff and attempting to keep ants and thieving hands out of the supplies.

'Yes, Mama, it seems very nice.' She felt drained, useless, and unable to make even the simplest decision or answer the easiest question. Monee and Romala, two of her married cousins, were looking lovely as usual, one in a vivid vermilion sari, the other in white and gold. They gathered her up, obviously delegated to take care of her.

'Come along, Victoria, we're going to walk into the trees. It's so much cooler there.' Romala slipped her arm through hers and pulled her along. Victoria hadn't the energy to protest.

Monee added her persuasion. 'Lunch will not be ready for a long time. Plenty of time yet for a cooling walk in the jungle.'

The musical cadence of their chatter washed over her. She didn't want to go anywhere, but found herself propelled along by the two determined cousins. They walked beside the riverbank to find Hector and Jit, yet more potential suitors, fishing. Even their friendly teasing failed to rouse her.

They strolled towards a grove of trees, which cast an invitingly deep shadow, about a quarter of a mile away. These turned out to be lime trees and Monee led the way into the centre of the cluster, holding back the boughs laden with small green fruit with one hand.

'In here, can you see that there's something hidden in the vines?' Monee asked.

Victoria ignored her. She had begun to feel strange, as if her head was disconnected from her body. From a distance she heard Romala squeal with excitement.

'Do look, Victoria, it must have been hidden here for centuries.'

She looked and saw they had entered a small glade in which there was a white shrine – a lovely vine-covered temple whose ancient columns had crumbled gently with age. It conveyed a powerful aura of tranquillity in the dappled sunlight. It seemed to be beckoning to her.

She collapsed beside it, too tired to walk further, the stone rough against her cheek. She was over-whelmed by grief. Life seemed too long to live alone. She wanted to slip quietly into dark oblivion where she would be able to rest. Clutching the small stone she let the peace of a religion much older than hers embrace her. Noise faded and she drifted into a quiet world where nothing could harm her. Her world shook, but she resisted and stayed within the blanketing darkness, slipping deeper and deeper away from harsh reality.

Voices intruded on her peace, voices she recognised, voices she loved. Reluctantly she allowed herself to be peeled from the rock and was vaguely aware of her father gathering her into his arms and holding her against him. Dimly she heard her mother's voice, soothing and reassuring. She remembered nothing of the journey home.

* * *

Henry vaulted from his saddle and ran into his commanding officer's rooms. He'd received an urgent message to return to barracks and thought his recall to England had arrived. This was the only reason he could think of for being summoned like this. If one of his parents had died there would be no need for such urgency. The news would be stale by now; whatever had happened in England, his presence, or lack of it, would make no difference. No, it had to be orders. Nothing else made any sense.

He skidded to a halt in front of the corporal who

guarded the inner sanctum of Colonel Caruthers. He saluted clicking his heels together. 'Captain Hindley-Jones, reporting as requested.'

The soldier nodded. 'Colonel says you're to go straight in, sir. He's expecting you.'

The door was ajar and he strode in and saluted a second time.

'Sit down, Captain. I need to talk to you.'

Puzzled, Henry snatched up a plain, straight-backed chair and sat facing his commanding officer, wondering what this was all about.

'I have a letter here for you; it's come from Delhi, from the high commissioner himself. I am to leave you in peace to read it.'

The high commissioner? What the bloody hell was this about? As far as he knew he'd never met the man. Why should someone so important send him a letter that had had him dragged back from patrol to read it?

He ripped open the envelope to discover a second unopened one inside. Frowning he tore this apart glancing at the bottom to see it was signed Victor Edward, Rajah of Marpur.

Dear Captain Hindley-Jones,
  When you visited a few weeks ago and

asked for the hand of my daughter in marriage I had no other choice but to refuse. You understood how things are, that in the present circumstances I cannot be seen to allow my daughter to associate in any way with the British, especially a British soldier.

However, sometimes political beliefs must be put to one side when the life of those one loves are at risk. Victoria is desperately ill. She has collapsed, and the doctor says she hasn't been eating and is physically weak. My daughter is pining for you and, reluctantly, my wife and I have decided to give our consent to your marriage.

This will mean, of course, that she can no longer be a part of our lives, that she must become completely English, or your career, and mine, will be destroyed.

Your commanding officer has no idea of the contents of this letter. He has been informed that you are to be given compassionate leave as your fiancée, Victoria Browning, has arrived from England and is unwell. I am in the process of obtaining false documents for Victoria. This will enable you to obtain a British passport for her once you are *married and her mixed ancestry will never be revealed.*

I have obtained a special licence for you also, so when you arrive at Marpur the marriage can take place as soon as Victoria is well enough.

I regret the circumstances that have forced me to write this letter, and hope you will forgive me.

Good God! Victoria was ill? Possibly on her deathbed? It did not seem possible that love for him had pushed her into a decline of this magnitude. The poor girl had not had anything to distract her – he had immersed himself in his work and, most of the time, had been able to ignore the pain of his disappointment. As the weeks had passed he had begun to believe it was for the best, that she was far too young to leave her home and marry him. He'd convinced himself they would both be better off marrying within their own circle.

He stared at the letter in his hand. It was amazing what could be achieved when you knew the right people. The rajah was obviously calling in favours and pulling strings. He pushed both envelopes into his jacket pocket. There was no time to waste. He was committed now, whatever his earlier reservations. Victoria needed him; if she was prepared to give up everything for him, then he must push his doubts aside and do the right thing.

Outside the corporal handed him a slip. 'The colonel said to give you this, sir. You have two weeks' leave.'

Two weeks! When he returned to his bungalow he would be a married man, bringing back a bride far too young to be the wife of a serving soldier. He loved her, wanted to marry her, but would she be able to live with her decision? Be able to give up her family without regrets for a man she'd met only three times?

* * *

Victoria woke several days later in her own bed with her mother seated quietly beside her. Too tired to talk she turned her head and smiled. A refreshing drink was spooned between her cracked lips and then she slept again. So she hovered, halfway between life and sleep, being baby-fed when awake, being watched and prayed over whilst she slept.

Sometime later, she never knew how long, she was disturbed by heavy footsteps approaching the bed. The murmur of male voices encroached on her peace; one her father's, the other she didn't, for a moment, recognise. Then a hard, calloused hand raised hers and she heard her name called softly.

'Darling, Victoria – wake up. I'm here to see you.'

Still believing she was dreaming she remained in the strange twilight world. Then the voice became authoritative, demanding she open her eyes at once. Startled awake she opened them and to her amazement, and delight, saw her beloved Henry sitting beside her, his blue eyes fierce, his jaw unshaven.

'Henry? Is it really you?' Her voice was thin from lack of use. 'How are you here?'

Holding her thin hands between his, he smiled. His eyes were wet. 'Your father sent for me. I've been given compassionate leave.'

Her father? Victoria glanced over his shoulder to see her parents standing pale and anxious behind him. Did this mean they were to be allowed to marry? Her mother caught her eye and nodded, smiling. Her father's head dipped, but his lips barely moved; it was more a grimace than a smile.

'Thank you, Mama, Papa; I know how hard this must be for you, but I don't think I could have survived without my beloved Henry.'

It was as though his return had opened a door and let her out of the dark room she had been hiding in. Her appetite returned and within days she was on her feet, incandescent with happiness.

Her parents, fearing first for her sanity and then for her life, had changed their minds. By agreeing to her marriage they were going to lose her, for she would move into a world in which they could not follow. Their explanation for their change of heart was that at least they would know she was alive and happy, and that would be enough for them.

Henry had only a few more days' leave and their wedding was hurriedly arranged. Papa had acquired a special licence and they were going to be married in the family chapel. She could hardly believe she was soon to become Victoria Hindley-Jones, the wife of an English officer, and Victoria Bahani would no longer exist.

She had made her choice. She was going to leave her past behind, start a new life with her English husband, although this meant she might never see her parents again. She understood the risk they were taking by allowing her to marry out of the family. Her father could lose his prominent position in the community if her defection was thought to have been with his blessing.

Only by severing all connection between them would they all be safe. She would no longer be part of an extended family. To make this marriage successful she was going to abandon the traditions she had adhered to all her life, learn to believe she truly was an Englishwoman. Learn to live with lies. Her parents would have to distance themselves from her, pretend they had no daughter.

She should have spent her last night as Victoria Bahani filled with anticipation and joy, but her heart was being torn apart. She had been forced to make an impossible choice. In order to be with the man she loved she must reject her family. She prayed long into the night that her decision was the right one, because after she said her vows in the morning, there would be no going back. The break from her family would be permanent.

5

MARRY IN HASTE

Papa had arranged for the family chapel to be built to allow Mama to pray when she wished. A priest from Bombay came out occasionally to conduct a Eucharist service. It had always seemed odd to have to drop everything and rush to the chapel, regardless of the time or day, when he arrived. The Hindu temple, which had been there for generations, was directly opposite and the only person bothered by this proximity was the English priest.

After considerable debate it was decided the wedding would take place in the evening when it would be less conspicuous. They would leave the following morning. This gave Victoria very little time to organise her trousseau and try to repair the ravages her nervous collapse had wrought.

Henry and she were now positively encouraged to spend time together in order to re-establish their relationship. The only place they could be sure of not being overheard was in the garden.

'Are you quite sure you want to go through with this, Victoria? You will be giving up so much to marry me.'

'I'm certain I'm doing the right thing. I belong at your side, wherever that might be.' She blinked back tears. 'Things will be much harder for my parents. I wish they had other children to ease the pain of my departure. Please, dearest, let's not talk about this any more. Tell me about my new home.'

'I have a bungalow in the British enclave along with the other officers. To be honest, I spend more time in the officers' mess than I do at home.'

'I have no domestic skills, Henry. I hope I shall not be expected to cook and clean. I have been taught to run a household, not to do the menial tasks myself.'

'Good God, no, of course not. I have a family of natives who take care of me very well. You can spend your time at the club – all the wives gather there.' He frowned. 'There's something we have not discussed. When I get recalled to England you will have to live with my parents in Essex. Not ideal, but I will be away with my regiment and I want to be sure you're safe.'

Victoria saw her mother beckoning on the veranda. 'I must go; I expect there are more clothes to fit. I pray we don't have to be separated too soon.'

He cupped her face and kissed her gently. 'I have some letters to write. Only a few more hours and you will be my wife. I can't promise it will be easy, my darling, but I will do my best to make you happy.'

Whilst she stood being prodded and poked by the seamstress, her mind wandered. The Rookery was a house completely run by electricity – what a novel idea! She liked her dancing lamps and staggering fans, all powered by paraffin.

When she wasn't with Henry she was with her mother sorting out her wardrobe, or with her father discussing the political and military situation she would have to face in Europe when she eventually had to move. Victoria could not decide what to wear for the ceremony. She had hundreds of saris and traditional outfits to choose from, but these somehow no longer seemed appropriate.

She was reading in her apartment when her mother came in, a garment over her arm.

'Good, I thought you had retired. Here, my darling, I wonder if you would like to wear this tomorrow evening.'

She held out a floor-length, cream satin creation, cut on the bias to give the skirt movement. The fitted bodice had a modestly scooped neck and elbow-length sleeves.

'Mama, that's perfect. Simple and elegant – is this what you wore when you married Papa?'

'Yes, it is. I can hardly believe this was my wedding dress. Try it on, my dear; see if it fits you.'

The gown fitted perfectly. 'Thank you, Mama, this is exactly what I wanted.'

'Excellent. We shall have a photographer present; your new family will think it odd if you don't have a record of such a special occasion. Now, put away your book and go to bed. Your father and I have planned for you to spend your last day on a picnic with us. Captain Hindley-Jones will no doubt have plenty to occupy himself in your absence.'

'Goodnight, Mama, and thank you.' She couldn't complete the sentence. The door closed softly, leaving her alone for the last time in her familiar bedroom. How could her parents remain so calm? She must emulate them – tears on either side would make leaving so much harder.

How strange to think her mother, all those years ago, had made a similar choice to hers. She had escaped from the dull world of middle-class England, from being a penniless governess to join the exotic, lavish life of the rajahs. Victoria was reversing the process – leaving the wealthy, aristocratic world and joining the lower ranks of England. She prayed her transition would be as happy as her mother's.

It had always seemed strange that even as a lowly governess her mother had more status in the eyes of the colonials than her father. He was a rajah – wealthy, powerful and respected throughout his community – but would always be *a native* to those who ruled his country.

Now Mama had become a moth fluttering around the light of her life, the rajah. Even her clothes were subdued, designed to blend into the background. She had never adopted the flamboyance of the Twenties. Victoria wanted to remain a colourful butterfly, to fly free in a new world. She shivered. Was she destined, like her mother, to live her life through her husband and be restricted by his world?

Mama had advised her not to pack any saris, which had given her another flicker of unease. If she was to fit in she had to hide the fact that she was Anglo-Indian, and proud of it, and appear to be wholly

English. For an instant she had hesitated. Was her love for Henry strong enough to reject all she stood for: her family, her traditions and her past? Certain it was, after all she had almost pined away when denied it, she closed her eyes to any doubts and packed the few European garments she possessed.

He father was going to give her a generous allowance, to be sent discreetly through an English bank. An army captain's pay was not enough to maintain her, in his opinion, and from this she could buy as many new outfits as she needed.

* * *

The early evening ceremony in the chapel was brief; no hymns, no sermon, just a hurried, almost furtive, exchanging of vows witnessed only by her parents. In the current political climate both Henry and her father had thought it best not to advertise the fact that the only daughter of a rajah was marrying an Englishman. They were to have a small celebration held in the house, which her mother had arranged.

'Well, darling – it's too late to change your mind. You're mine now. I promise you'll never regret it.'

Victoria tried to smile but her mouth refused to respond and uninvited tears spilled down her cheeks.

Ignoring her parents, hovering behind them, Henry stopped, pulling her almost roughly into his arms.

'Sweetheart – don't cry. Listen to me. I know how hard this is going to be for you. You've got to give up everything you've ever known – swap your life of luxury for that of an officer's wife. Ignore what I just said. If you have the slightest doubt – say so – the marriage can be annulled. I'll leave and you'll never have to see me again.'

His urgent words resounded with sincerity. Victoria felt as if her heart was swelling. 'No! Never! I love you; I have no regrets – no doubts. I really don't know why I'm crying.'

Impervious to their surroundings, and the many interested faces of the servants, he tilted her face and she received her first kiss as a married woman. When his lips covered hers all her fears evaporated and a delicious warmth flooded through her. Reassured, and confident she had made the right choice, indeed the only choice, she placed her hand in his.

On the arm of her new husband who was resplendent in his dress uniform, tall and strong, the equal of any man present, she almost floated across the lawn and into the house. Family and friends were gathered in the hall. Her appearance was greeted with a muted round of applause and, smiling, Henry and Victoria led the way into the huge, gloomy dining room. For this special night political differences were put to one side.

This was true Victorian grandeur, everything large and opulent, the dark wood polished and dusted, and gloomily smug. Each heavily ornamented leg of the vast central table stood in its own glass saucer, a protection against the ever-present ants. The floor was a sea of purple and gold carpets and dappled panther skins – scarlet-edged – were strewn everywhere.

From the heavy sideboards Aladdin lamps threw shadows upon the islands of furniture and the light rebounded from rich, red-papered walls on which dark brown wall paintings made deep and mysterious holes.

The table itself sparkled; candles gleamed from solid silver candlesticks and flashed upon cruets, decanters and cutlery, in brilliant self-satisfaction. The company was dispersed around the table, a boy at each chair to seat the guests. She had pride of place at the head, Henry beside her. Her parents sat on either side of them; then uncles, aunts and cousins. This was a family event – no neighbours or friends had been invited. This was the first time she had seen the table full. There must have been more than fifty people arranged round it.

Her mother, who had chosen tonight to appear in a blue and gold sari, plaited her long hair and put on heavy silver earrings, looked as though she had been born here. She directed the servants and the conversation simultaneously. This was where Mama belonged, among the saris and long gloves, the bracelets and earrings that tinkled as they ate. Victoria realised that as she had become an Englishwoman her mother had finally become an Indian.

The meal was as grand as the room. Two peacocks dominated the buffet laid out on a long side table. These were plentiful enough in the area but, in order not to offend the religious beliefs of some of the local people, the birds were smuggled tactfully into the house and dealt with by the hunters themselves.

She sat in her elegant European wedding dress, next to her new husband in his British uniform, surrounded by vibrant saris and high-necked black jackets. Victoria realised, sadly, she was no longer part of this world. Her marriage had, like her mother's so many years ago, effectively severed all ties. From now on she belonged with Henry, and would have to learn a new way of living, a new set of rules and customs.

She had made her decision and by choosing to marry the man she loved had willingly given up her heritage and her parents. She prayed that she would find Henry's family as loving and kind as her own.

They left before dawn the following morning. She had said her goodbyes the previous night and asked to be allowed to leave without an audience. She wanted to look forward with joy, not back with tears. The luggage was stowed silently in the boot. Henry stood apart, giving her time to have one final glance around. She was glad it was almost too dark to see. The sounds of faraway animals and the raucous cry of a peacock were the last things she heard. The call of a peacock would always make her cry.

Henry took her hand and gently drew her into his now familiar embrace. With his arms around her she knew she had made the right choice. Eager to leave, she was the first to scramble into the car, not waiting for either her husband, or the chauffeur, to offer assistance.

It was quite extraordinary that she was going to live scarcely two hours' drive from her home and both her father and mother regularly visited Bombay, but she would be unable to communicate with them. Her life would be untenable if ever a hint of her mixed ancestry became known so she must pretend she had no family.

Her father had arranged for a fraudulent birth certificate to be made on which her maiden name had become that of her mother – Browning. She could use this if ever it was necessary to confirm her false background. She was glad her wedding certificate was genuine. At least she could read this to confirm she had once been Victoria Bahani, not Browning.

She didn't consider it wrong, or racist – this was just how things were. You couldn't live in both worlds. Once her mother had made the choice she had been accepted, totally – no patronising, no unpleasant nudges or sly reproaches. She became a Bahani. Now Victoria must do the same and even though she had given up far more than her mother, she believed her marriage was worth it.

The pale sunlight flowed across the empty park, chasing them as they drove away. She closed her eyes to the trees, silhouetted against the sky, ignored the intricately carved wrought-iron gates as they passed through. Her eyes were firmly forward.

Henry and her father had decided it would be advisable for them to stay, for the remainder of his leave, in a good hotel in Bombay. She couldn't wait to step up to the reception desk and be introduced as Mrs Hindley-Jones. She had already decided never to wear gloves again; she wanted everyone to see the shiny, new gold band.

Bombay *is* the Raj Hotel, the Army and Navy Stores and the railway station. Victoria Terminus was big enough to hold a festival in. The car stopped under the immense white portico of the Raj. The uniformed doorman salaamed before opening the door. She exited as gracefully as she could, finding the unaccustomed freedom of the mid-calf skirt of her silk dress so much easier to move in than a sari.

The chauffeur, Victoria supposed she ought to have known his name, unloaded the luggage and handed it over to the boys, smartly dressed in white. She slipped her shaking arm through Henry's and smiled up at him. He pressed it. Then they followed the obsequious doorman into the noisy reception hall.

This was like an aviary. Groups of chattering people broke and reformed between the potted palms. White, green and indigo turbans bowed and swooped like startled birds as friends greeted one another with uninhibited pleasure. Sari-clad women embraced tenderly and waved braceleted arms. They called out, cried out, sang out, as the mood took them. The whole babble rose above the noise of the whirling fans.

Little knots of sober-faced, panama-hatted men lay in long, oddly shaped cane chairs, drinking from ice-filled glasses that tinkled pleasantly as they were lifted or put down. For the first time she was no longer a part of this crowd. Walking proudly beside Henry to the desk she imagined she really was an English bride, and this her first time in India. She smiled wryly – it was fortunate she'd always liked play-acting, for she would be living a lie the rest of her life.

At the desk Henry was presented with the book and registration slip. He was required to state their nationality. He didn't hesitate. *British* was written in both sections with a flourish. It was done. So simply, with one word, she had crossed the line, become British. No one would question her ancestry now.

Of course none of this would have been possible if her father, like all the eldest sons of the once pro-British rulers, had not been educated in England, called to the bar and spoken English straight from the Cambridge Backs and Lincoln's Inn. Her English was impeccable also. Schooled by both her parents, she had never been allowed to develop the sing-song cadence of her cousins. She was thankful for their insistence now, as this would immediately have identified her as an impostor.

The room that was to be her home for the next two days was vast, but not unfamiliar. The mahogany bed, isolated under a mosquito net, was an invitation neither of them could resist. In the centre of the room, directly over the bed, the large propeller creaked and groaned, through various pitches, adding an accompaniment.

Lovemaking, as her husband called it, was a pastime she could happily spend all day investigating.

'Darling one, much as I would like to stay here, we have shopping to do.'

She pushed herself upright allowing the sheet to slip enticingly. 'Must we? Could we go tomorrow instead?'

He chuckled. 'Sorry, my darling, this afternoon it has to be. We must allow time for any alterations that might need doing.'

'Is this a tactful way of suggesting I need to remedy the discrepancies in my wardrobe?'

'It is, sweetheart. Anyway I thought all women loved to shop.'

The bed dipped as he stood up, politely keeping his back to her as he pulled on his clothes.

'Is there time for me to have a bath before we go?'

'Of course; I shall wait downstairs for you. I'll arrange for a car to be outside in say... an hour? Shall I organise something to eat as well?'

'Yes, they do wonderful sandwiches here. I'll be down in thirty minutes. That leaves plenty of time to eat before the car arrives.'

She watched her husband of less than twenty-four hours stride out. He only had one gait: soldier-straight and march! She wondered if he walked in a more leisurely fashion in civilian clothes.

Not wishing to linger in the rose marble bath-room, she made do with a stand-up wash in the enormous bath, which was sufficient to remove any smell of bed activity. She couldn't bear for anyone else to suspect what they had been doing, however normal it was for newly married couples.

Downstairs one of the ever-present boys escorted her to a seating area away from the bar. It was almost noon and there were several other groups eating an early lunch. This room had not the slightest whiff of spice or exotica – no Indian food allowed in this strictly European domain.

Victoria glanced round nervously. She was worried she would be discovered and sent packing before her guide led her to Henry. At least there was no danger of her being recognised in here. Henry was already on his feet, his smile so wide she forgot her fears and almost ran into his welcoming arms.

There was only one place to shop in the whole of Bombay. When the car stopped outside the Army and Navy Stores one could have been visiting the town hall. They were ushered between the high marble pillars by a gigantic, red-turbaned Sikh, and her heels clattered noisily as they passed from one silent, high-ceilinged department to another.

There were many assistants, all European, but very few customers. First they bought some remarkably dull floral dresses, and then sensible shoes and three dinner gowns. Victoria's favourite purchase was a daring black velvet dress, very décolleté at front and back, relying for its limited modesty on slim diamante straps. She could never have worn this at home.

Next they moved to the toiletries section. Henry, telling her to call him to sign the chits, took himself off to a group of chairs centrally placed in the great room, and sat, with great aplomb, looking at nothing. The counters were set at least twenty yards apart, providing gentle exercise and more than enough privacy for a lady's little boudoir secrets. Her purchases were parcelled and carried out to the patiently waiting chauffeur and they returned through the heaving streets to their hotel.

All too soon it was time to leave and for Henry to return to duty. Victoria already knew she was to live in a spacious bungalow, in the British quarter a short distance from the barracks. He promised he would return when he was able, but as a serving soldier his life was not his own.

How she was to fill her days she had no idea; Henry had talked vaguely about women's groups and tennis partners and officers' clubs that she could attend, but obviously had no intention of introducing her himself. Socialising was not high on his list of priorities. The disturbing news from Europe about the activities of the German chancellor, Hitler, and an Italian commander, called Mussolini, were of far greater importance.

The taxi slowed and they entered a wide, tree-lined street, with identical low white buildings on either side. They were set up above the road and reached by a short flight of pristine white steps. She caught glimpses of emerald grass, bougainvillea and jacaranda-covered verandas before they halted halfway down the street. The taxi hooted loudly.

'This is it, darling. We're home,' Henry said, and leant across to open the door. 'The housekeeper will take care of you.' He almost bundled her out. Before she had time to adjust she was left, surrounded by boxes and bags, alone on the side of the road, watching her husband of three days drive away without a backward glance.

He didn't turn his head to wave; his eyes were to the front, his mind already on his duties. She realised then that however much Henry loved her, she was always going to come second. He had placed her firmly in a small compartment labelled 'wife'. His real life was the army. She would just have to learn to fit in.

6

FINAL FAREWELLS

Some time passed before Victoria felt completely comfortable in the bungalow and even longer before she felt brave enough to venture out to the club where bored wives met to drink copious quantities of gin and it, and swap tasty bits of gossip.

Henry was a wonderful loving husband, when he was home, which was seldom enough. On one of his infrequent visits they were sitting on the veranda before dinner.

'Henry, I wish you could come back more often. I have no one to talk to. Why has no one called round to introduce themselves?'

'I asked them not to call, darling. I rather thought you would prefer to adjust to your new life for a few weeks before you had to entertain strangers.'

'I see. I thought I was being ignored for some reason. Presumably it is usual for a new wife to be welcomed into the community?'

'Of course it is. I can't understand why you won't go to the club. If you can shoot a panther without a blink surely you won't allow something as insignificant as an army wife to intimidate you?'

'My real fear is that I will inadvertently slip up and reveal my background, ruin your career and our marriage by one mistake.'

'You have to be brave, sweetheart. You will be incredibly lonely if you don't get out and make some friends. Dressed as you are and with your hair up you look as British as I do. I feel dreadful I didn't make it absolutely clear my duties keep me away from home much of the time.'

'I promise I will go soon, but not tomorrow.' A slight noise behind her made her slop her drink. 'Good, dinner is ready. Shall we go in?'

It was sheer boredom that finally drove her out of the house; she had nothing to do apart from read, paint or sew. Her father must have visited Bombay several times during this period, but she might as well have been in Calcutta as they could not meet. She was desperately homesick and longed for the comfort and conversation of her extended family.

The house was kept immaculate by the servants and the meals were all prepared for them. The garden lovingly prinked and pruned by another small army of helpers. Victoria never discovered where they came from, or went to, but the house-keeper and her family lived in a small shack behind the kitchen. She never went there, but sometimes wondered how so many could fit into such a small space.

Eventually she decided she could hesitate no longer. Tomorrow she would put on her best frock, order a taxi, and go to the club. She woke feeling de-cidedly nauseous and almost changed her mind. But she was not going to let nerves defeat her, not today.

Dressing carefully in one of the dreadful cotton frocks and unflattering shoes, which Henry had in-sisted were *de rigueur*, Victoria felt far from confident. Henry had promised he would be home that evening and she was determined that this time she would have something new to talk about.

Her taxi was not coming until ten o'clock and she had got ready far too early. It was cooler inside but she decided to sit on the veranda where she could smell the heavy perfume of the jacaranda and orange trees growing around the bungalow.

On scanning the newspaper, thoughtfully ordered by Henry, she read about the desperate goings-on in Germany and was filled with foreboding. The problems with Congress and Home Rule seemed trivial by comparison. Several regiments had already departed for England; this news meant Henry was almost certain to be called back soon.

The British Indian Army, in which her grandfather had been an officer, would be left to keep order here. She had a horrible premonition that the days of peaceful, non-violent protest, started by Gandhi, were rapidly departing.

The hoot of the taxi reminded her it was time to go. Worrying about this outing seemed silly when there were so many worse things going on in the world. The taxi driver would have to find somewhere to park so that he could wait until she reappeared. No doubt he would fill in the time smoking beedis and chatting.

The interior of the club was cool and quiet; only the softly whirring fans, the distant sound of women's laughter and tinkling ice cubes to disturb it. Swallowing hard she headed briskly towards the laughter. Victoria emerged, blinking, onto a shady veranda on which a group of assorted European ladies were sitting; some in tennis gear, others in dresses identical to hers.

As one their heads turned and a dozen pairs of eyes focused on her. She swallowed hard, again. For some reason she felt horribly sick. She was going green and became desperate to find a lavatory before she disgraced herself in front of those she hoped to make her friends.

A hand grabbed her arm and someone spoke. 'Quickly, my dear, come with me.' She was rushed through a door and into the restroom just in time. Her breakfast violently reappeared, thankfully in the privacy of the cubicle.

When she came out, pale and shaky, she found her rescuer leaning nonchalantly on a wash basin, unbothered by her illness, smoking a cigarette in a long amber holder. She introduced herself with a charming smile.

'Feeling better? I'm Fleur Montague. You must be the elusive Victoria Hindley-Jones. When we heard that the gorgeous Henry had finally succumbed we were consumed by envy. He's an absolute dish. No wonder you've not bothered to come and see us here.'

'I'm so sorry. What a way to arrive. Thank you so much for getting me here in the nick of time.'

Fleur waved a languid hand. 'I know morning sickness is absolutely ghastly; I was sick as a parrot for the first four months with Miles. Oh, the joys of having a baby!'

Victoria looked at her in astonishment. 'Pregnant? Is that why I'm feeling so sick? I had no idea I could be having a child so soon. We've only been married seven weeks.'

Fleur pushed herself upright, grinning widely. 'Good God! Victoria, it need only take one night. Did your mother not tell you anything?'

Her eyes filled. 'No, my parents are dead. I was raised by an elderly friend of my father's.' And as she told the lies Henry and she had concocted to cover her apparent lack of family, she felt a hollowness inside. With one casual sentence she had wiped out her home and her heritage.

'My dear, I'm so sorry. Absolutely ghastly. Come and sit down in the powder room; it's cool and quiet in there. You need a long drink of water to steady your nerves and settle your stomach.'

By the time Fleur had explained the mysteries of conception and the horrors she could expect at the birth, they were firm friends.

'Are you feeling well enough to meet the others?'

'I am, thank you. I need to use the restroom again. I seem to be in and out all day at the moment.'

'Yes, that's another delight of pregnancy.'

A few minutes later they stood, side by side, in front of the mirrors. Fleur was the perfect foil for her darkness and slender frame. She was tall and statuesque with clouds of fluffy, ash blonde hair. Victoria thought she was wonderful.

'I am ready now, Fleur. Are the other women as nice as you?'

'Absolutely not, my dear.' She laughed at her expression. 'Don't look so scared; I will protect you. It's not personal; any girl as young and lovely as you is going to cause the green-eyed monster to arise. And having snaffled the most eligible bachelor in the regiment is another black mark against you.'

Victoria swallowed hard and, with her new friend, sailed back into the fray. Luckily Victoria's dramatic arrival had effectively broken the ice and the assembled women all greeted her with sympathy. When she returned home, an hour or so later, she was laden with invitations to lunch, tea, tennis and cocktail parties. She was assured she could attend with or without her husband. This group of wives had long ago learned if they waited for their partners to escort them anywhere they would rarely go out.

She had also been given several remedies for morning sickness, which ranged from ginger, to the leaf of a tree she had immediately forgotten the name of. At least there would be far more to discuss with Henry than just a visit to the club.

Exhausted by her excursion she retired to bed for the remainder of the afternoon. Henry was not expected home until six o'clock which gave her plenty of time to have a much-needed sleep and still be able to dress and bathe before he arrived. He arrived home far earlier than expected and she was still in bed when he burst into the bedroom.

'Darling, I'm sorry to disturb you, but it can't wait.'

Groggily she sat up. One look at his face was enough to tell her it was grave news. 'What is it, Henry? Have you been recalled?'

'I have. I've got to leave on the next ship. We only have two days' embarkation leave, then I shall be confined to barracks until we leave in four weeks' time.'

'Two days?' She scrambled out of bed forgetting her own momentous news as she tried to absorb his. 'What about me? What shall I do if you're gone?' She tried to keep the pain from her voice but failed miserably.

'Darling girl, it will be all right.' He gathered her close and slowly her pounding heart returned to normal. Henry would take care of her; he always did. His hands smoothed circles of comfort around her back creating a welcome warmth. Slowly this changed to a different kind of heat and they tumbled backwards on to the bed. Such was the urgency they made love without him even removing his boots.

'Bloody hell, what was I thinking of?' He rolled away swinging his feet to the floor as he buttoned his trousers.

'Please, darling, don't apologise. It was quite exciting. Was that what is called "a quickie"?' Victoria enquired, trying to keep the amusement from her voice.

His head shot round. His eyebrows were so far up his forehead they almost disappeared into his mop of fair hair. She collapsed into a fit of giggles and was quite unable to speak.

'You're incorrigible, Victoria. Wherever did you hear that word?' His tone was affectionate and he pulled her into his arms, stroking her sweat-stained hair back from her face.

'Sorry, darling. But I've been to the club today. I met a lovely girl called Fleur Montague, and well, you know how it is when married women get talking.'

'I don't, actually, but I can imagine. Did you enjoy yourself?'

'I did. I wish I'd plucked up the courage to go earlier. Now it's too late. Everyone will be going home.'

'Not immediately. Plenty of time to continue your friendship.' He kissed her then reluctantly stood up. 'Look, we have to talk. Don't worry about getting dressed; come out on to the veranda as you are. I'm going to shower and get into my dressing gown as well.'

'I need one too. Shall we have one together?'

He shook his head, laughing. 'Absolutely not! You stay there, sweetheart; I'm going in first.'

She listened to the sound of water falling and her eyes dripped in sympathy. In two days her beloved husband would be gone – only to the barracks, but away from her. She would have to learn to live on her own until her departure to England.

She froze as a horrible thought shook her. Was she to go with him? Surely British wives and families would not be left behind without protection with anti-British feeling running so high? Her stomach rebelled and, ignoring Henry's instructions to stay out of the bathroom, she flew across reaching the lavatory just in time.

Retching over, Victoria drew a shuddering breath.

A cold damp flannel was pressed into her shaking hands.

'Here, darling, wipe your face. Shall I get you a drink to wash out your mouth?'

She nodded, too exhausted to answer. After filling her mouth with water she spat into the bowl. Henry closed the lid and pulled the chain. Carefully she began to push herself upright.

'No, I'll carry you.' Without waiting for her reply he scooped her up and took her into the bedroom. She didn't need to tell him her news; he had guessed.

'You're pregnant, aren't you, sweetheart?'

'I am. I didn't realise until today. I've been sick every day for the past week but thought nothing of it. And it's several weeks since I had my course.'

'Are you happy about it, darling? It's far too soon. I should have taken more care. Good God! You won't be eighteen until June.'

'Lots of women have babies far younger than me. I'm thrilled, honestly I am. Having a little Henry or Henrietta will give me something to think about when you're far away and can't come home to see me. But you haven't said – are you pleased?'

'I'm delighted, of course I am, but it does present a problem. All wives and families are scheduled to sail back as soon as the troops have left. It will be wretched for you on a ship when you're already so sick.'

Eventually it was decided she should spend some of the small fortune her father had given her to pay for a seat on an aeroplane. That way she could accomplish the journey in a little over three days.

* * *

The next weeks passed in a frenzy of cables, phone calls and packing. She still found the time to visit her new friend and spent several happy afternoons in Fleur's company. Her husband was not in the military, he worked for an Anglo-Indian Company, and they were not, at the moment, being repatriated. It was unlikely they would meet again for a while. However, the girls exchanged addresses and promised to write to each other.

Victoria wrote to her parents telling them about the pregnancy and the date of her departure. She was in turn too sick or too excited to worry about the impending upheaval. She was to fly out the week after Henry. His parents had been instructed to collect her from the airfield.

Everything was taken care of, no detail left undone. Mr and Mrs Hindley-Jones would transport

Victoria back to their home where she was to live until Henry could provide alternative accommodation. It would be nice to live with Henry's family, but it bothered her that maybe she was just exchanging one set of parents, and their rules, for another. On his final morning at the bungalow she broached the subject.

'Henry, are you sure that your parents are happy to have me to live with them?'

'Of course they are, darling, I'm their only child and you are my wife. Ma always wanted a daughter so she will be thrilled to have you there especially as you're carrying her first grandchild.'

'I'm worried they will expect me to act like a daughter rather than your wife.'

He laughed. 'It's quite different being a daughter-in-law. You're a married woman, a mother-to-be; this gives a status you've not had before. Don't worry about it, sweetheart.'

'It's going to be horrible separated from you for so long. I can't believe the next time we meet will be in England.'

'I know, but we have to be strong. I promise I'll come and see you in Essex as soon as I get leave.'

The staff car hooted from the road. She flung herself into his arms, unable to bite back her sobs. 'I can't bear it. Leaving India is going to be hard but having you leave me is even worse.'

'I must go, darling girl. Be brave for me and the baby. I'll come to you as soon as I can.' His eyes glittered; he was equally distressed. She couldn't let him go believing she was in shreds.

'I shall be fine, my love. I'm just emotional because I'm pregnant. Hurry up, don't keep your car waiting. I'll see you soon. I love you. Take care of yourself until we meet again.'

He brushed her wet cheek with his finger, nodded and strode off. She stuffed her fist in her mouth. She wouldn't break down in front of the servants; that would never do. He jumped into the car, turned briefly to smile and raise his hand, and then he was gone. God knows how long it would be before she saw him again.

Although she wasn't leaving for another week she would still arrive before he did. She would be safely ensconced in Essex several days before his ship docked. She prayed their love would prove strong enough to survive the upheaval.

7

FLIGHT TO ENGLAND

The thought of travelling halfway round the world in a large metal tube with wings, and being forced to spend three days and two nights in hotels en route with a group of people she had never met, while suffering from morning sickness, did not fill Victoria with joy. However, where Henry went, so must she and her journey was going to be much more comfortable than his.

Once aboard the Fokker Trimotor aircraft at Karachi, she realised she was destined to get to know her fellow passengers pretty well before they finally landed in England. The seats were set in pairs on either side of the narrow aisle, their high backs ensuring in-flight privacy. There was no way to get a general view of the company, but there was a girl sitting next to her and, rather nervously, Victoria introduced herself.

'Hello, I'm Victoria Hindley-Jones.'

The girl smiled back. 'I'm Joan Thomas. Are you travelling alone as well?'

'I am. My husband's a captain in the British Army and has been recalled to England. He left last week by troopship.'

'Golly! You don't look old enough to be married.'

Victoria laughed. 'Not only married, but I'm expecting a baby in November.'

'Poor thing! I'm married to an Indian – at least I was – I'm going back to England to get a divorce. I should have realised chalk and cheese don't mix. What seemed exotic and magical to a naive twenty-year-old turned out to be something alien and unpleasant.'

Victoria nodded, encouraging her to continue. Joan curled a strand of her russet hair round her finger and closed her eyes for a moment.

'My mum warned me. She said an English girl wouldn't fit in with their heathen ways.' She looked up, her green eyes sombre. 'Sorry, they're not my views. I'm not bothered by religion either way. No, it wasn't that, it was the fact I was put to one side in the women's quarters, not expected to do anything apart from looking ornamental and being ready to... well... you know what, whenever my husband appeared.'

'I'm sorry you have been unhappy here. I love India. It's where I grew up and it's breaking my heart to leave it like this.'

Impetuously Joan reached across and squeezed Victoria's clenched fists. 'Don't get me wrong, I love the country, but I can't live here independently. I'm going home to do my bit. Nurses are going to be needed once the war starts.'

'You're a nurse? Is that how you met your husband?'

'It is. He was visiting London when he broke his ankle and I was on duty when he was admitted.'

Their conversation was forced to pause whilst the remaining passengers, who had the seats directly behind them, fussed and grumbled their way past. Their seats were towards the rear of the craft, in the tail, and she could see the plane was almost full. The air stewards started checking the overhead luggage lockers and began to hand out charcoal biscuits and boiled sweets so departure must be imminent.

'I think we're almost ready to take off. Have you flown before, Mrs Thomas?'

Her companion's mouth curved. 'Joan, please,

and it's Miss Thomas. I'm not using my married name any more. Thank God my passport hadn't been altered. And, yes, I flew out here. One thing I was never short of was money.'

Victoria thought it was going to be wonderful having an experienced traveller next to her. 'I'm terrified. I can't believe that hundreds of tons of metal can fly safely through the air. I'm so glad I'm sitting next to you; having someone to talk to will help take my mind off things.'

As the engine roared the aircraft rocked and her stomach rebelled. Joan held open an in-flight sickness bag and without a qualm sealed it neatly when Victoria had finished.

'I don't envy you, Victoria. Flying with morning sickness will not be pleasant. Have you tried anything to stop it?'

Victoria wiped her mouth. Joan was so calm, so matter-of-fact about everything; it must be because she was a nurse. Maybe this flight was not going to be so bad after all. 'I've got some cold ginger tea somewhere; that works sometimes. And now I've got these charcoal biscuits, maybe they'll help.'

They didn't. It seemed that their part of the plane was in a perpetual spinning motion. She was grateful the pockets in front of her contained a generous supply of air-sickness bags.

She was surprised to see a woman steward, but maybe things were different in Holland. In spite of her frequent nosedives into a paper bag, by the time they touched down in Alexandria, Joan and she had become the best of friends, albeit temporary. She had told Victoria several amusing stories about her nursing experiences and made her almost envious. Whilst Joan would have a crucial role to play in the forthcoming struggle against fascism, she would have to be content with being a mere spectator.

'The Egyptian airport is, like all of its kind, international and anonymous,' Joan told her.

'I don't care what it's like; I shall just be glad to be out of the plane and on firm ground again.'

Victoria suffered the momentary illusion that she had spent the past hours circling around Karachi only to return there. 'Good grief! I see what you mean, Joan. We could be back in India again. I had expected Egypt to be different, more exotic somehow.'

'It's a shame we don't have time to go and look at a pyramid or a sphinx,' Joan said as a porter and bellboy escorted them to their rooms.

'Never mind, perhaps we will have time to explore at our next stop. I'm going to have a bath and change my clothes. Shall we meet in the lounge in an hour?'

'Are you sure you feel well enough? You've been terribly sick the whole flight. Don't you think you'll be better having a tray in your room tonight?'

'Absolutely not. I've paid the earth for this ticket and I'm going to make the most of every moment. And I feel perfectly fine now we're not airborne.'

She was pleased to discover the rooms were air-conditioned and the water clean and fresh. Once changed and bathed she was ready to join her new friend downstairs.

The lounge echoed hollowly. Theirs was the only plane to make an overnight stay and they had the hotel's facilities to themselves. As the only, apparently unattached females both of them were soon encircled by a number of young men who were all fellow passengers. Victoria ostentatiously flashed her wedding ring and introduced herself as Mrs Hindley-Jones.

The young men were remarkably polite. She touched Joan's arm. 'My husband told me everyone gets very jolly in the evening and they drink far too much. Why aren't these chaps enjoying the free drinks? Why are they all acting so prim and proper? It doesn't seem at all natural.'

'Now you come to mention it, you're quite right. Alcohol is usually irresistible to the male of the species.'

Everything became clear when they were joined by the rest of the passengers who had, during the flight, been hidden from them by the seats. Victoria would have seen these people earlier in the day, when the aeroplane had refuelled at Basra and most of the passengers had disembarked to eat and use the sanitary facilities provided, but she had fallen asleep. Joan said that she had looked so peaceful she hadn't the heart to wake her up.

They had discussed the fact that their aircraft was making so many detours. It had flown over the old city of Babylon; the captain himself had come back to point out the supposed site of the Garden of Eden and the passengers had also been flown over the principal places of the Holy Land, including a rooftop view of the city of Jerusalem. This may not have been routine, for the latecomers into the lounge were very important people indeed.

Most of them were middle-aged and indefinably august. 'Who are the VIPs, do you know?'

One of the helpful young men was ready with the

answer. 'The Governor General of Australia and his wife are the couple in front. The smart woman is Lady Mountbatten; I believe she is returning from an official Red Cross visit to Sydney. Apparently she's been presented with a pet wallaby.'

'Heavens! No wonder everyone is on their best behaviour.' Victoria turned back to Joan. 'That explains all the detours and the captain appearing so often.'

Also included in this party was a cluster of generals and senior diplomats from Singapore. They and their ladies created an island of solid respectability at which the young men cast wary and envious eyes. The ladies, without exception, were dressed in floral gowns and genteel stoles. The men were in informal mufti. It occurred to Victoria she had never seen Henry out of uniform, out of clothes, of course, but not in civilian garb.

'Look at that, they've brought the wallaby to dinner,' Joan said.

'The poor captain has been given the honour of looking after it. Doesn't he look uncomfortable? With all that kicking and struggling I expect it'll be hopping all over the lounge very shortly.' Victoria smiled as the animal was handed from one set of blue-clad arms to another. Authority had its privileges, and his second officer inherited the burden.

The airport dinner was literally inedible. At the sight of the horrible Europeanised kebab, all fat and gristle, her stomach lurched and she excused herself quickly from the table. The diplomats and soldiers did not flinch; they were tucking in with every appearance of satisfaction. All the men at the table stood politely. Joan stood up too.

'Are you unwell, Victoria? Shall I come upstairs with you?'

Hand clamped firmly over her mouth, she shook her head. Joan nodded, understanding immediately. 'I'll look in on you later; make sure you're not feeling too bad.'

Victoria heard the chairs scraping as the table reseated itself. By the time she reached the foyer, away from the revolting food, her nausea calmed. She paused at the massive reception desk to collect a soft drink and a packet of arrowroot biscuits before retiring to bed.

When Joan tapped at the door she was wide awake and eager for company. Her new friend had consumed several glasses of wine and was only too happy to entertain Victoria with her experiences.

* * *

Late the following afternoon they were crossing the Greek Islands on the way to their next night's stop at Athens. The sea was a deep, unforgettable, cerulean blue, and before them lay the hallucinatory green of the land. Victoria had never seen such vivid grass before.

They were ushered to an airport bus, which was to take them to their hotel in the centre of Athens. 'I should like to tour the city. I've read so much about Athens in my father's Greek classics. Will you come with me, Joan?'

'I should love to. Anyway, I wouldn't let you go on your own – not when you're so sick most of the time.'

The bus rumbled to a halt outside the hotel. 'I hope we have adjacent rooms again, Joan, then you can call in for me when you're ready.'

Less than an hour after their arrival Victoria was in the vestibule with her friend. Joan had no difficulty hiring a taxi and a guide. She thanked God for Joan; she would never have attempted such a venture on her own.

'Where do you want to go to first, Victoria?'

'I should like to see the shopping centre first, if you don't mind.'

This was acutely disappointing; any bazaar at home offered more variety and at better prices. Nor did she find the Greeks themselves particularly friendly or attractive. They all wore shiny black and seemed to be short, broad and sweaty. Her long-held image of men like gods walking through a timeless land was shattered.

'Golly, this taxi is hot. Shall we go and see the Acropolis next? You look a bit peaky, Victoria. Are you sure you don't want to go back to the hotel?'

'Absolutely not, I shall never have this opportunity again and I'm not going to miss it even if I vomit on the statues.'

As the taxi pushed its way towards the Acropolis it passed through areas in which poverty was displayed as openly as any seen in India. However, when she walked up to the Parthenon her neck hairs tingled with awe as she approached the Turk-battered temple. Here was a building to compare with her beloved Taj Mahal.

She leant against one of the great columns and the moon rose and flooded the landscape with mystery. The city lay dark at the foot of the hill and the cypresses and olive trees stood in silvered clumps on the ground between. She was exhausted by the time they returned to the hotel.

'You look done in, Victoria. Don't bother about coming down to dinner. I'll arrange for something to be sent up to you on a tray.'

'Would you? That is so kind. Why don't you join me? Unless you want to spend another evening being ogled at in the dining room.'

'I certainly don't. You go up and have a nice long bath. I'll do the same then come along to your room in about an hour.'

'That'll be lovely. Let's hope the food is more palatable here. I think I'd like something cold – cheese sandwiches would be wonderful.'

'I'll ask for fruit and soft drinks as well. See you in a while.'

That evening's meal was much more suited to her jaded palate. As they ate Joan explained why she'd become a nurse and Victoria was fascinated.

'Can anyone train or do you have to have special qualifications?'

'I matriculated from a grammar school, but I think there's an aptitude test you can take instead. The interview is more important than the exams you've passed. And if there is a war, which seems very likely, I think they'll be desperate for women to come forward for training.'

Victoria sat back, feeling comfortably full for the

first time since she'd left her lovely bungalow in Bombay. 'If I wasn't happily married and pregnant I'd definitely become a nurse.'

'Look, I'll give you my home address. Will you keep in touch? I'm intending to join Queen Alexandra's Nursing Corps when I return so I'm not sure where I'll be posted. This is part of the army; it means I'll be doing my part for the war. But you can write to me at my parents' address and they can forward your letters.'

'I'm going to be living with my in-laws. They have a house called "The Rookery". It's in a small village called Mountnessing, near Brentwood, which I believe is in Essex. I've no idea whereabouts in England that is, but somewhere north of London, I think.'

They parted with fond embraces. Tomorrow would be their last day together. Victoria really liked Joan and was determined to stay in contact. Having a friend in England would make her feel less lonely and help to lessen her homesickness. Tomorrow they were to refuel at Sofia and Munich; then would come Amsterdam and the short hop across the North Sea to Croydon and from there to Essex to meet her new family.

* * *

Five o'clock in the morning was an unsociable time, especially if, like Victoria, you were suffering from morning sickness. Even Joan was strangely subdued. All the passengers were grimly silent.

Quite obviously many were still feeling the effects of the previous evening. She fervently hoped the pilot had had a sober and early night; the rest of the crew were looking decidedly wan, which their dark glasses only served to emphasise.

Later they floated down through the cumuli and arrived at Munich. What greeted them there was totally unexpected. As the plane taxied to a halt Joan, whose turn it was to sit in the window seat, gasped in shock.

'Oh my God! There are armed soldiers running towards the plane. I think the war must have started. We are going to be interned.'

Ripples of unease were travelling round the plane, but nobody panicked, nobody screamed. British men and women always presented, so Henry had told Victoria, a stiff upper lip. She knew this meant she had to face whatever happened without showing her fear, but the thought of being locked away in a German prison camp was almost too much for her.

'It's going to be all right, Victoria. You mustn't get

upset; it's bad for your baby. Whatever happens I'll look after you. I've delivered loads of babies safely.'

Joan's comforting words were enough to soothe her. The stewards were hurrying along the aisle attempting to reassure the passengers and reminding them that if they remained dignified and didn't panic they would be treated with respect. Germans, they were told, appreciated the British reserve.

Both doors were opened and the metal stairs were in place far too quickly. Storm troopers appeared at either end of the aircraft and gestured with their guns. They forced the passengers to disembark. They were herded into a waiting room and armed guards took up their stance outside the door.

There had been an ominous development. The German authorities had little goodwill to show. She and the other detainees sat around in silence, drinking coffee. She was terrified war had actually been declared and she would be taken away at any moment.

There were newspapers lying about and Joan, surprisingly, announced she was able to read German and volunteered to try and find out what was going on. There were threats and warnings directed at most of the nations on the continent; the Poles seemed to have attracted the most venom. The group perceptibly relaxed. The generals agreed, quickly but with authority, that Hitler was turning in the right direction.

The date was the fifth of May 1939. Victoria knew little about Poland, nothing about the corridor and did not know where Danzig was. She remembered, however, her uncles had declared their belief that other people's danger would provide India's salvation.

A good deal of coffee was drunk before they were herded out of the lounge and marched smartly back to the waiting aircraft. For her part she was quite prepared to run flat out if it would get them off the ground and out of Germany any faster.

8

THE ROOKERY

There was no one to meet Victoria at the airport. She waited, surrounded by her expensive leather suitcases, for over half an hour before deciding she had been forgotten.

She knew that she needed to get to 'The Rookery', Mountnessing, near Brentwood, Essex. Surely this couldn't be too difficult? After all she had just travelled halfway round the world on her own. She stiffened her spine and adopted her father's clipped English accent.

She demanded, rather more stridently than she had intended, that someone get her a porter immediately. Instantly she was approached by a uniformed person of indeterminate age. She explained that she needed a taxi to Essex. She had no clear idea where this place 'Essex' might be but felt sure she had more than enough English money to cover the cost.

Ten minutes later she was handed aboard a large black vehicle with shiny chrome headlights and a rear end that looked remarkably like the hood of a perambulator. Thankfully the interior was relatively clean.

Her cases were strapped beside the driver with much puffing and muttering, which surprised her. At home drivers and porters were only too eager to work. Eventually the man was satisfied and climbed back into the cab. The dividing window was already open and he half-turned to ask exactly where she wanted to go.

When Victoria told him he almost got out and removed her cases. It seemed Essex was rather more than double his usual run. Reluctantly he agreed to take her if she agreed to pay for his return journey. England looked very like Holland and the brisk breeze and watery sunshine were certainly the same. The streets were all paved, the people healthy, but dully dressed. But where was the smell that told one you were in England? In India the air was spicy and warm, redolent with blossom and people's lives.

The sun looked small and faraway, its rays weak

and its warmth imperceptible. She wondered if she would ever adjust to the vagaries of the British climate. She liked to know when it was going to rain; in England, Henry had told her, it fell randomly, regardless of the season.

The taxi springing did not help her delicate digestion and the English countryside passed by mostly unremarked. Victoria was forced to close her eyes and concentrate on not disgracing herself. She wished she had had the foresight to bring some of the convenient paper sacks from the aircraft.

Finally, thank God, the vehicle slowed down and she was able to sit up. They had drawn up in a tree-lined country road, in front of a large building with a hanging sign reading 'George and Dragon'.

The driver turned and smiled sympathetically. 'Not far now love. You hang on; I'm just popping in to the pub for directions.'

Her distress had obviously been noted and softened the driver's attitude. Minutes later he returned, a broad grin on his whiskered face. It seemed 'The Rookery' was no more than two miles away. She felt a little better now and looked out of the window, eager to see the house that was to be her next home.

The vehicle turned right up a small lane and then sharp left between two pillars into a gravelled, semicircular drive. It stopped in front of an attractive, yellow-brick, double-fronted building. A flight of wide stone steps led down to the sweeping gravel. The driver opened the rear door and it was with considerable relief she stepped out.

This was where her beloved husband had been born, where he grew up, where she was to live and where, in six months' time, their first child would be born. The front door, navy blue, with a brass knocker in the shape of a gargoyle, remained closed. No one had noticed her arrival. This was not an auspicious start and a wave of homesickness almost swamped her.

The taxi driver was busily unloading the luggage, which left her to announce herself. Her misery was replaced by anger. Henry would not be pleased at her reception and neither was she. She marched up the steps and banged on the door. There was the sound of hurrying footsteps and the door was flung open by a flustered young woman in a black dress and white apron. The look of absolute horror on her face would remain forever etched in Victoria's memory.

'Bloomin' Nora! Mrs Hindley-Jones, however did you get here?'

'I waited for over an hour then arranged for that

taxi to bring me here. Can someone bring in my luggage, do you think?'

'You go on in, madam. I'll sort out your cases and pay the taxi driver. I hope he told you how much it would cost before you set out?'

Victoria shook her head. 'No, I'm afraid I didn't ask.' She delved into her handbag and gave the maid her wallet. 'Here, I'm sure there is enough in this.'

Unwilling to enter the house unescorted she hovered on the top step watching the lively altercation between the servant and the taxi driver. Finally an amount was agreed upon and the taxi drove off leaving the luggage marooned on the gravel.

The girl picked up two of the bags and staggered up the steps grinning. 'What a cheek! Right villain he was. He would have charged you double the going rate, but I soon sorted him out. Go along inside, madam. I'll fetch Tommy to carry the rest of your things.'

On the way upstairs the girl, Madge, told her Mr and Mrs Hindley-Jones had, indeed, gone to the airport to collect her. At least the contretemps had broken the ice.

'Here you are, madam, this is the room the captain uses when he's home. I don't see how the master didn't find you. Never mind, you got here safe and sound.' The girl dumped the cases on the floor. 'Why don't you have a bit of a sit-down and I'll fetch you a nice pot of tea. Then I can unpack for you.'

'Thank you, that would be lovely. If I could have a slice of bread and butter to go with it I would be most grateful.'

By the time her belongings were installed in her new accommodation Victoria was relaxed and able to laugh at the catalogue of errors. It appeared that she had left too early and her in-laws had arrived too late.

The maid, Madge, chatted away as she unpacked the clothes. She admired the frocks and costumes, evening gowns and dresses. Victoria was glad Henry had persuaded her to purchase such an array of uninspiring garments. They were obviously exactly right for her new life. Madge told her she would need 'a couple of cardies' as it was 'a mite chilly' in the evenings and Victoria promised she would get some. Exactly what it was she needed she had no idea.

The rooms prepared for Henry and Victoria were adequate, but not what she was expecting. Henry had told her that his parents were wealthy and the biggest landowners in the area. But the rooms were cold and poorly furnished.

The sitting room had a bare, polished wooden floor with a small blue rug isolated in the centre. On either side of an inadequate fireplace were armchairs covered in a faded blue velvet with cushions that dipped in the middle. The large window seat, with lumpy red padding, looked even less appealing. The bedroom had an enormous oak wardrobe, a matching kneehole dressing table and a brass bedstead with a sagging mattress.

Disappointed and dispirited she wanted to weep. If this was all a wealthy family could afford then poverty in England must be worse than at home. It was some time before she discovered that the upper middle classes in rural England preferred to live like this. She never really understood why they considered creature comforts so unimportant.

* * *

Two hours after her arrival Mr and Mrs Hindley-Jones turned up. From her vantage point on the window seat Victoria saw their grand car arrive and watched them get out. Henry's father looked nothing like him. She noticed, as he turned round to open the door for his wife, that his frame was slight, his hair grey and his posture stooped. Mrs Hindley-Jones, however, was everything she'd expected. She was a magnificent woman, far taller than Mr Hindley-Jones, and everything about her was extravagant.

She instantly looked up and beamed and waved expansively. Victoria couldn't hear what she was saying clearly, but her booming voice was a perfect match for her statuesque figure. She almost ran downstairs. She knew she was going to love Mrs Hindley-Jones; Henry looked just like her.

They met in the entrance hall, amongst the dreary aspidistras and huge, dark brown portraits of long-dead ancestors. Mrs Hindley-Jones enveloped her in a hug that took her breath away.

'My dear girl, I cannot apologise enough for this dreadful welcome. We quite mistook the time your flight was due to arrive and you had gone by the time we got there.' She stood back holding Victoria by her arms, scanning her face closely. 'I can see exactly why Henry fell in love with you. You are exquisite, but far too young to be married and having a baby. Still – too late to worry about that. I intend to take care of you whilst my boy is away. Anything you want, anything at all, you only have to ask.'

'Thank you, Mrs Hindley-Jones. Madge has looked after me and my belongings are already unpacked.'

'Please call me Marion, my dear. I want you to feel completely at home here.'

The enthusiasm of her welcome more than compensated for the miserable arrival. Marion was everything Victoria had prayed for, and more. Henry and she were going to be happy living here until they could find a place of their own.

* * *

'Marion, Henry will be coming home tomorrow.' Victoria waved the letter that had arrived that morning.

'That's excellent news, my dear. I know he's busy, but I did expect him to put in an appearance before this. Leaving you alone for three weeks is just not good enough.'

'I'm certain he would have come before this if he could. I'm glad we've got a day's notice. That will give me time to wash my hair and so on.'

'I shall ask Cook to make a cake and a sherry trifle to celebrate. Would you mind very much if I invited a few close friends over to meet you? I can't tell you how eager everyone is to see Henry's beautiful young bride.'

'I know I should have been coming to church

with you on Sundays, but whilst I'm so sick in the morning it's just not sensible.'

'Never mind, my dear girl. Everyone understands you're in a delicate condition. This horrible morning sickness usually passes by four months. Surely you must be that already?'

Victoria smoothed her blouse over her small bump. 'I must be almost that, I think. I suppose I'd better make an appointment with the doctor and get all that sorted out.'

'You didn't answer my question, Victoria. Do you think you and Henry could spare us a couple of hours on Saturday afternoon? I promise we won't intrude on your precious time any more than we have to.'

'I should love to meet your friends, Marion. I have the perfect dress – one I've not yet had the opportunity to wear.' She smiled at her mother-in-law. 'I want to wear it before I'm too large.'

When Henry arrived in a borrowed car his parents had already gone out for the day. Even the staff were busy elsewhere. Victoria flung open the front door, dashed down the steps and threw herself into his arms.

'Henry, I've missed you so much...'

'I know, my darling, I should have written more

often. Let me look at you – yes I can already see the difference. You definitely look pregnant now.' He slung his canvas kitbag over one shoulder and put his arm around her waist. 'Where's Ma and Pa? They usually can't wait to see me.'

'We have the house to ourselves until dinner time. They thought we would like a little privacy as we haven't seen each other for so long.'

His eyes darkened and his fingers dug into her waist. 'Shall we take an afternoon nap, sweetheart?'

She nodded. 'I just hope I'm not ill this afternoon. I can't imagine why it's called *morning sickness* when it happens on and off all day.'

'You poor thing; no wonder you look as if you've lost weight when I expected you to be blooming.'

They spent a blissful day making love and swapping horror stories of their travels. They also discussed baby names and where they would eventually live. Germany's occupation of Czechoslovakia was not mentioned, neither was Chamberlain's warning that further attacks would meet with resistance. They both knew war was inevitable now and their time together limited.

Henry had joined the Essex Regiment, which was on high alert and could be sent abroad at any moment. A junior British officer still led from the front, and Victoria had read enough about the 'Great War' to understand what this would mean.

'We must get up, Henry. Your parents will be home soon.'

'I shall run you a bath, darling girl. You stay where you are until it's ready.'

He marched across the chilly linoleum without bothering to pull on his dressing gown. She loved the way his arms and legs moved in perfect coordination even when stark naked. It must be because of his years of marching on parade.

Henry's reunion with his parents was muted. No hug even from Marion, and from his father he received a handshake. The British were very strange; no doubt the unreliable climate and appalling food contributed to their lack of emotion.

* * *

The next day six friends of her in-laws were to come for afternoon tea. She and Henry went up to change at three o'clock. 'I'm looking forward to meeting some of your parents' friends, darling. And I actually like afternoon tea – it reminds me of home.'

'Food here takes a bit of getting used to, I expect.

By the way, have you heard anything from Fleur, or the woman you met on the journey over?'

'Nothing from Fleur – I expect she's en route somewhere by now. Joan has written to me and I've replied. She promises to come and see me if she gets posted near enough. I should love to see her; I've met no one my own age here.'

She turned her back so he could zip her dress. 'As you haven't been out anywhere, sweetheart, that's hardly surprising. As soon as you're feeling better at least you can go to church and so on.'

The sound of footsteps on the gravel outside ended the conversation. Henry checked his boots were shiny and his tie straight. She rubbed her face against his rough khaki jacket. 'Why didn't you wear a suit today? There are half a dozen in the wardrobe.'

'Against the rules – could be court-martialled if caught in mufti.' He grinned and lifted her from the floor. 'I thought all girls love a man in uniform.'

'I much prefer you out of it.' She pulled his head down and kissed him wishing, they could tumble back into bed and forget about afternoon tea.

Victoria was so on edge she was unable to eat anything. Fortunately everyone thought it was because of her condition and didn't insist she try the cucumber sandwiches, scones or cake. She found it surprisingly easy to pretend to be one of them – English, a girl who just happened to have been born in India. She would never remember their names for the women were all but identical and the men exactly like her father-in-law. Her afternoon tea dress was perfect and much admired by the ladies.

'Well, my dears, that went splendidly. You ate nothing at all; Victoria, why don't you go and lie down and I'll have Henry bring you a tray in an hour? There will be no dinner tonight. I thought perhaps we could have Welsh rarebit later on.'

'I shall do that, Marion. This will give you time to catch up with Henry and his news.'

* * *

After Henry left, Victoria was prostrate with sickness and misery for several days. The unrelenting rain did nothing to alleviate her sadness. She shivered and retched in the uncomfortable bedroom and had never felt so alone.

June 10th was her eighteenth birthday. The dawn chorus woke her and, enchanted, she got out of bed and went to the window. Every tree seemed filled with music. She watched the sunrise, bathing the lawn with light, warming her as she crouched, face against the glass, feeling well for the first time in weeks.

It was her birthday; although she was the only one, as far as she knew, who was aware of this. The start of her new year was as good a time as any to finally put her past away and embrace the role of an English wife, deep in rural Essex.

Summer slipped by; after all the shouting and table banging nothing much happened on the war front. Children who had been evacuated from London, and other major cities, began to drift back home and the threat now seemed very far away from her peaceful existence at The Rookery.

Henry, stationed at Colchester, was able to come back occasionally. Usually he caught the train, but sometimes managed to cadge a lift. Victoria slowly adjusted to what was expected of her. But everything in Essex appeared subdued; the sun, the landscape, the clothes, and especially the food, which was uniformly revolting. Even voices and emotions seemed repressed.

She was supposed to be an English girl who had been born in India. Her father had explained precisely what marrying Henry would mean. If his superior officers ever discovered he had married a half-caste he would be demoted and ostracised. The sooner she became accustomed to her new life the better. Of course, the baby would be born British and would be the sole heir to a small fortune and a huge house. She just wished Henry and she could find a place of their own where they would be able to relax and not have to watch every word.

And the lies! They had invented a history for her with conveniently defunct parents, but every day Marion, or one of her friends, would ask for more details. Victoria was drowning in prevarications and deceits, and because of this there was a danger she would eventually become entangled in her own web and the awful truth would come out.

Then Hitler invaded Poland and two days later, September 3rd, war was declared. Henry got twenty-four hours' compassionate leave before vanishing, newly promoted to major, overseas. His letters were all she had to sustain her. But Arthur, her father-in-law, kept saying, 'It will all be over by Christmas; don't worry about it, my dear.'

She was glad she had the impending birth to think about. Henry, or Amelia, was due on November 17th, but everyone, including the midwife, said the baby was more likely to be late than early, as it was a first one.

Petrol rationing had been introduced and train

journeys were discouraged. Blackouts were erected on the windows and gas masks issued, but apart from that nothing much was happening. Henry's battalion had not been engaged in any fighting and he was quite enjoying his enforced stay in France.

In the early hours of November 15th she went into labour and Amelia Jane was born, a satisfactory seven pounds. The in-laws would have preferred a grandson but she was delighted with her new daughter. A telegram was immediately sent to Henry. The birth was, she was told by the midwife, very easy. She hated to imagine what a difficult delivery would entail.

She thought it had been like trying to push an orange up her nostril. By the time her beautiful daughter arrived she was exhausted. But the baby was worth every minute. A perfect baby. Soft dark hair framed her oval face and huge, dark blue eyes. Her complexion was pale, much more like Henry than her mother.

* * *

Christmas 1939 would be Victoria's first as a wife and mother and she was determined to try and enjoy it. Marion was going to so much trouble, and both she and Arthur missed Henry as much as she did. She would never forget the candlelit tree or the carol-singing round the piano whilst the fire, piled high with sweet-smelling apple logs, crackled its accompaniment. Outside there was deep snow, very festive, but she hated it.

Sore breasts and broken nights were forgotten as the magic of a traditional English Christmas swept her along. She hoped her darling Henry enjoyed the Christmas parcel he had been sent, which had included a beautiful photograph of their daughter taken and developed by Stanley, a neighbour's son.

Amelia was to be baptised in the New Year and the various relatives were staying on to celebrate this. There was obviously no point in waiting for Henry; they all realised it could be months before they saw him again. The baptism was to be held in the freezing church on the first Sunday after Christmas, immediately after Morning Prayer. The thick covering of snow might make the countryside sparkle in the wintry sun but Victoria detested it. In fact she hated the cold; it seeped inside her clothes and sapped her strength. How she longed for the warmth of her homeland. She was grateful she was allowed to travel in the pony cart, as she had the baby to carry.

The rest of the party crunched happily through

the snow. After all, it was scarcely over a mile to the little Norman church and her new family loved to walk, and ride, however inclement the weather.

Henry should have been there. A stranger held his daughter in his place. Marion kept saying to Victoria, 'There's a war on, my dear,' or: 'We are all in the same boat, my dear.' This was true, but it didn't make her feel any better.

The introduction of rationing suited Marion's need to do something. Fires immediately became even smaller and the food even more unpalatable. The weather was freezing and foggy, and after an initial thaw, the snow returned with a vengeance. Even if she'd wished to, she could not leave the house. The Home Service news bulletins announced the snow was feet deep all over Europe. Poor Henry, away from home and up to his armpits in horrible, wet, white stuff. She felt dispirited and lonely throughout the grey months of winter, and even Henry's long passionate letters failed to cheer her.

Her beautiful daughter thrived, however, so at least she was doing something right. By May, Victoria had thawed out and Amelia was crawling, had sprouted her first teeth and was universally adored, especially by Arthur. The baby's grandfather had formed a unique bond with her and spent almost as much time with Amelia as she did. As the baby flourished, so did he.

His posture became more upright and his eyes brighter. It was as though Amelia had switched on a light inside him just as Henry had for her in her other life, back in India. Watching him with her daughter was heart-rending, knowing her own father would never have the chance to meet his granddaughter.

When, on May 10th Winston Churchill replaced Neville Chamberlain as prime minister, Arthur was jubilant. He honestly believed with Churchill in charge Hitler would be defeated and Henry would be able to come home.

It had been necessary for Amelia to transfer to the bottle as the stress of Henry's absence had caused Victoria's milk to dry up. Nanny had been resurrected from retirement and the baby's welfare handed over. She began to feel redundant. Her protests were ignored. Far better for baby to have 'a routine', and Victoria was needed to help Marion with her many war efforts. She became an expert at winding bandages and knitting balaclavas. When Mrs Smythe asked for volunteers to do a first-aid course her hand was the first to go up.

Marion was not impressed. 'My dear Victoria,

why ever did you put your name forward for the first-aid course? It will mean going away for a week and you will have to leave Amelia. Henry would not approve of his child's mother being away.'

'Marion, you know as well as I do Amelia is perfectly happy with Nanny and Arthur. And I spend so little time on my own with her now she's weaned. I want to make myself useful, and they will need qualified first-aiders once the bombs start to drop.'

Marion frowned at her, unconvinced. 'That's as may be, my dear, but a woman's place is at home with her child, war or no war. We promised dear Henry we would take care of you; how can we do that if you're away from The Rookery?'

'I'm sorry, Marion, but my mind's made up.' Victoria smiled up at her. 'Unless, of course, you get rid of Nanny and allow me to take charge of my daughter?' She would abandon her decision in a second if this was agreed to.

'Don't be silly, dear. Send Nanny packing? Whatever next! Henry was most insistent Nanny look after Amelia. It's how things are done over here, you know.'

Victoria was losing her baby and there was nothing she could do about it until Henry came home to support her. She was being robbed of her maternal duties by a frosty-faced elderly woman, a stranger to her and her baby, but no one else thought that this was wrong.

The English had barbaric customs – at home all the children from wealthy homes had their own ayah, but she was there to help, not take over the up-bringing of the child. Victoria froze as something un-pleasant and unexpected occurred to her.

Things were not really so dissimilar at home. Women handed their babies over to be looked after by servants; it was only in her house, because her own mother had been a governess, that things had been arranged differently.

'In which case, Marion, I shall do the first-aid course knowing my daughter is in excellent hands. Henry would not want me to sit idle when there's a war on.'

That clinched it. The slightest suggestion that anyone could possibly be shirking their duty to King and Country and her mother-in-law became outraged.

'Very well, Victoria; you have my blessing. Did Mrs Smythe tell you when the course is to take place?'

'Next Monday; but she'll give me the details at the next WVS meeting.'

* * *

The week-long course was exactly what she needed to take her mind off Henry. Victoria loved the discipline and was told she had an aptitude for nursing. She couldn't wait to write and tell Joan, who was working in a London hospital, that she now had a certificate saying she was qualified to administer basic first aid. This was her very first qualification and she was thrilled with it.

Towards the end of May they sat, as usual, around the wireless waiting for the news. It was grim. Germany's earlier invasion of the Low Countries had taken everyone by surprise, but they believed their superior forces would hold them easily. How wrong they were. Hitler's troops stormed through Holland and Belgium and now France itself was fighting for its life. The British Expeditionary Force was seeing action of the most fearful kind.

Marion reached over and squeezed her hand, but no one said what they were all thinking. There must have been thousands of desperate prayers said that night all over Britain. Her nineteenth birthday was rapidly approaching and this year she decided to mention it. It would at least give them a new topic of conversation.

Marion was mortified to think Victoria's last one had been ignored and thought a small celebration with invited guests would be in order. When it was pointed out that there was nobody to invite, apart from the mainly middle-aged women Victoria had met at the WVS meetings, this idea was dropped.

She had made no friends in the village; there were older wives, with whom she had nothing in common, but the unmarried girls of her own age were all volunteering for war work. She was stranded between two groups and belonged to neither.

Eventually, with relief all round, the plan for a party was abandoned completely. No one was in the mood. The news bulletins were not encouraging; they gave little actual detail, but Victoria could fill in the blanks easily enough. In this case 'no news was bad news'. Information was sketchy but everyone knew something dreadful had happened at Dunkirk.

* * *

When the scale of the heroism of the people of Kent became known she prayed Henry had been one of the lucky ones; that he would prove to be amongst the thousands who had been rescued from the beach.

Her birthday passed again, unremarked. She still hadn't heard from Henry. Arthur had pulled all the strings he knew, contacted every person who might have information, but still they had no official news of Henry. She was already beginning to fear the worst when, on June 18th, she saw a boy riding a black bicycle, wearing a neat blue uniform, pedal slowly up the drive. Arthur was out shooting something, Marion was at one of her endless committee meetings. It would have to be her.

Somehow she forced her legs to carry her across the lawn, Amelia on her hip (it was Nanny's day off), protesting loudly at being snatched away from Teddy.

She intercepted the boy. He, unsmilingly, handed her the telegram and she watched, in a dream, as he turned his cycle carefully, remounted and pedalled away, apparently unconcerned he was leaving her world in tatters.

* * *

9

DEATH AND DESERTION

Victoria pushed the unwanted envelope into the pocket of her skirt. She knew what was inside. If she didn't read it perhaps the news could be ignored. Amelia wriggled and snatched at her hair, trying to attract her attention.

'Shall we go in and wait for Grandpa and Grandma, darling? Mummy has something to give them.' The baby gurgled happily, unaware she would never meet her daddy. Victoria felt her throat clog and swallowed furiously. Whatever happened, her beloved daughter would not be upset. She had to be strong – Amelia only had one parent now.

Inside everything seemed so normal. Madge was singing in the kitchen and Tommy banging about in the boot room. The grandfather clock in the hall struck twelve. As the last chime faded away it took her life with it. How was she going to live without Henry?

It was time to give Amelia her lunch and it would be waiting in the kitchen. Pinning on a false smile she walked down the long, uncarpeted passageway and pushed open the door.

The maid looked up with a grin. 'There you are, my little angel. I thought your mum had forgotten it was time for lunch.'

'Can I leave you to feed her, Madge? I have something I need to do.'

'Course you can, madam. This little duckie is no trouble at all. All smiles and no tears; you must be so proud of her.'

'I am. I don't know what I'd do without her.'

'I hate to think what will happen when you and the major move out and take the little one with you. She's given Mr Hindley-Jones a real spring in his step. I don't know how he'll survive the separation when it happens.'

Victoria wanted to scream that it would never happen; her darling husband would never come back to take them away, but something held her back. Somehow she managed to mumble an answer and fled from the room. She *had* to read the hated telegram.

Upstairs she scrambled onto the bed, drawing her knees up under her chin as she used to as a child. Her hand was shaking and she could hardly get it into her pocket. Eventually she pulled it out and tore it open. Her eyes blurred and she couldn't take it in. There were the usual platitudes, false sympathy, then the words she didn't want to see. Major Henry Hindley-Jones had been killed in action on the beach at Dunkirk.

Numb with misery, she was unable to move even when she heard Marion returning. She could hear her heavy footsteps hurrying towards her room.

'My dear girl, has it come? Mrs Smythe said the boy came here with a telegram.'

Mutely she pointed to the screwed-up paper on the bed. Marion didn't have to read it, she only had to look at her face. 'Victoria, my dear, I am so sorry. Here, let me hold you whilst you cry. You need to cry, my dear. It's nature's way of stopping you going mad with grief.'

* * *

The next few days passed in a blur. Victoria saw everything from a distance – as if looking down the wrong end of a telescope. She was experiencing a nightmare in which Henry had died and at any moment she would wake up and everything would be as it should be. Perhaps she would have recovered more quickly if Nanny had not decided Amelia should be kept away from her.

Marion and Arthur did everything they could to help her come to terms with her loss. It was only now she realised how much she loved them and how much they loved her. As there was no question of Henry's body being returned for burial, they decided to make do with a memorial service in the church. This was arranged without her participation as she was too wrapped in her own misery to think about anything else.

Ten days after receiving the telegram a letter arrived for her. If Marion had realised what it contained Victoria was sure she would never have brought it up. It looked innocuous enough. It was addressed in unfamiliar handwriting and had been posted in London. She thought it might be from Fleur as in her last letter she had said that she was about to embark for England.

She opened it carefully. It contained a single

sheet of lined paper and a second, smaller envelope. Curiously she picked this up wondering what the dark brown smudges on the back might be. She flipped it over and the hair on the back of her neck rose. She recognised the handwriting. This was from Henry. How could this be? Henry had been dead for more than two weeks. If she had stopped to read the note she would have understood immediately. But she didn't. With tears streaming down her cheeks, she ripped open her beloved's final communication.

My darling,

This is going to be the hardest letter I've ever written. By the time you receive this I will no longer be alive. The Germans are coming towards us at a frightening pace and I fear we will not be able to hold them back. The Maginot Line is a nonsense. We do not have enough troops or any air cover. I believe we will all be trapped by the sea, unable to retreat. It will be a miracle if any of us survive.

I shall not post this letter, but carry it close to my heart. If I die, I pray someone will take it back to England and post it on to you. The censors would never allow me to send it. I *hope, in the circumstances, whoever finds it sends it unopened.*

I love you, my darling girl, and I know how much you love me. But I am begging you not to grieve too long. You are young and beautiful – I want to meet my maker knowing you are strong enough to carry on alone, as so many other wives and mothers will have to.

We have spent such a pitifully short time together, but long enough for both of us to re-alise how lucky we have been to share a love like this. One day you will meet someone else and fall in love again. You have my blessing and I promise I shall always be watching over you and our beautiful daughter.

Goodbye, my love; take care of yourself and do whatever you have to in order to sur-vive this terrible war.

Yours for eternity,

Henry

As she read his last words of love and encouragement she felt a great weight lifting from her shoulders. Henry knew her so well. He wanted her to be strong and get on with her life without him and that was what she would do.

She picked up the accompanying letter and read it. A comrade, seeing him fall had stopped to attend to him.

Finding him dead, he had removed his personal possessions and identity discs. The personal items would arrive from the Ministry eventually but the Good Samaritan had done exactly what Henry had prayed for. He had kept the letter and posted it on when he arrived in London. He gave no forwarding address so she would never be able to write and thank him for his kindness. He would never know that his gesture had saved her sanity.

* * *

The days drifted into weeks and Victoria threw herself into her first-aid training. She was only able to spend an hour or so a day with Amelia as Arthur and Marion monopolised her. They were so brave. They had lost their only son but had, in those dreadful days, put Victoria's needs first. She owed them so much. How could she begrudge them the consolation of time with her daughter?

The loss of the channel ports meant Hitler was almost upon them. Churchill had made a rousing speech on the day before the telegram arrived. He had declared Dunkirk was their finest hour as they had turned a miserable defeat into a victory for British bravery and hope. How could the death of hundreds of thousands of men, and the loss of all their equipment, be called a victory of any sort? For her, and thousands of other wives and mothers, it was the end of happiness.

Somehow life carried on but she still felt as if she was walking two steps behind everyone else. The only time she could forget her loss was when she was busy at the hospital. She was now considered proficient enough to work alongside the real nurses. She no longer had to attend the WVS meetings; it was accepted that her war work was nursing.

Things continued in much the same way until in August she had an unexpected visitor. Victoria had just completed an early shift at the hospital and was almost too tired to cycle round to the back door and put her bike away. She could hear voices coming from the open kitchen windows and her spirits lifted. Joan Thomas had come to visit her at last. The fatigue of her day forgotten, she almost ran inside to greet her friend from India. It would be a relief to talk to someone who had never met Henry, someone from outside her circle of grief.

'Victoria, I hope you don't mind me coming down

to see you. I've got a week's leave and thought you might need cheering up.'

She rushed across and flung her arms around Joan as though she was a long-lost relative, not a person she'd known for three short days more than a year ago. 'It is so good to see you. Have you met my in-laws, or my daughter, yet?'

'No, I was told they have all gone for a picnic somewhere down by the lake. I'm hoping you're going to invite me to stay the night; if you do I can meet them when they get back.'

'I insist that you do. Can't you stay longer? A fresh face is just what we all need at the moment.'

'I'm afraid I can't. I must go and visit the parents as well. This is the first leave I've had since May. After the debacle at Dunkirk...' She stopped in mid-sentence, horrified she'd inadvertently reminded her friend of Henry.

'Please, Joan, don't look so worried. I'm over the worst – at least, almost over.' She turned to Madge who was listening to this exchange with interest. 'Have you got time to make up the bed for Miss Thomas? I know it's Cook's day off and you have to prepare the evening meal today. We can do it ourselves, if you're too busy.'

'Go along with you, madam, it won't take me a

tick. Shall I put her in with you? The single bed in your room has hardly been used.'

Victoria looked at Joan. 'Would you like to share? It would give us more time to talk if you do.'

'I'd feel lost on my own; everyone has to share a billet in the forces.'

'Right you are. I'll nip up and do it now, before I forget.' Madge grinned at Joan. 'You're lucky, miss – tonight it's rabbit pie and salad.'

'Sounds all right to me. Although I must admit the food in the canteen is not too bad.'

'Do you remember the ghastly meals they served in the airport hotels? I was amazed anybody ate it.' Talking about food reminded her how much she missed the spices and richness of her own cuisine. 'Shall we go and sit in the garden with a cold drink? I don't expect Arthur and Marion will be back until teatime.'

There were deckchairs already arranged under an ancient oak tree. The dappled sunlight filtered through the faded green, making the area beneath a sanctuary from the baking sun. After the worst winter in living memory they were now suffering a heatwave. At least, out here in rural splendour, they were protected from the worst of the weather. The house remained bearable, even on the hottest days, and one could always find a cool spot somewhere in the extensive grounds of The Rookery.

'Well, how are you coping, Victoria? You've lost too much weight, but your lovely dark hair is still shiny and thick.'

'Frankly, I still think it's all been a terrible mistake. That another telegram will arrive telling me Henry is not dead, that it was an administrative error. I'm only surviving by working. When I'm here I have too much time to think and the blackness closes in on me.'

'It's not surprising; it's only two months since you heard your husband died. It will be months before you can think about him without falling apart.' She sipped her squash, obviously choosing her next words carefully. 'You said in your last letter that you are now a nursing assistant at Brentwood Hospital. Have you considered training to be a state registered nurse? I know they're recruiting at the moment.'

Victoria stared at her. Was this some kind of joke? How could she leave her baby and go away to train as a nurse? 'Are you mad? I have responsibilities here. I can't possibly abandon my baby.'

Joan was not to be deterred. 'But, Victoria, you hardly see your daughter. Either the nanny or her grandparents have charge of her. I know from your letters your in-laws treat you like a child, not giving you any chance to make decisions. I wish you would reconsider. This is one way you can be independent. Your country needs you. The Germans are already bombing the factories and ports and air raids are expected daily in London. Your nursing skills are being wasted in a country hospital – the wounded will be in London.'

'I know that. I listen to the news and read the papers. But remember, Amelia never met her father. What you are suggesting is impossible. If anything happened to me she would be an orphan. Surely you wouldn't wish that on her?'

'If you weren't here, her life would continue as usual. She has loving grandparents and her nanny. She is living in the lap of luxury and that won't change. Victoria, you will never recover from your loss if you stay here to be reminded every day of how things could have been. You need to get away, start again somewhere else.'

Joan was only telling Victoria what she already knew. She had been thinking about leaving The Rookery and finding a house. Living on her own would mean she would no longer be treated like a child. However hard she tried to demonstrate that her actual age did not reflect her maturity, her in-laws persisted in the belief she was incapable of making decisions for herself and certainly not for her daughter.

Money wouldn't be a problem. She had more than enough in the bank to purchase several houses. The only thing stopping her from leaving was the knowledge that taking Amelia away would destroy her grandparents. Was Joan's suggestion so outlandish?

'You're right, Joan. I do feel trapped, smothered. I have been seriously considering taking my baby and going to live somewhere else, starting a new life for both of us, but I know Henry would want his daughter to grow up where he did.'

'There you are then. Come with me when I leave tomorrow. Make a clean break. You have two choices – stay here and watch your baby being reared by someone else, or leave. Either way is going to be difficult. But coming to London to start training as a nurse doesn't mean you'll never see your baby again. You get time off every month and can come down and spend quality time with her. Your in-laws will be proud of you and so will Henry.'

Victoria stood up, impatient with all the talk. 'Please, let's not discuss it any more. I need time to think. You don't understand what it's like being a mother. I have already lost my husband I don't think I could bear to lose my daughter as well.'

Joan left the next day without mentioning nursing again. Her friend was waiting to be sent overseas, and it was unlikely they would meet again until the horrid war was over. Victoria didn't have a shift at the hospital and was going to spend the whole day with her daughter. Talking about leaving Amelia had made her desperate to be with her and she was determined that neither Nanny, nor her in-laws, would prevent her.

As she climbed the stairs to the nursery she could hear her baby laughing. Her heart contracted at the very thought of leaving her.

'Good morning, madam, baby is getting ready to go out with her grandparents. I'm sorry, but you can only have five minutes.' Nanny smiled indulgently and busied herself collecting clean nappies and other paraphernalia.

Victoria smiled at her daughter and held out her arms, intending to take her away whatever plans Nanny might have to the contrary. But her lovely baby turned away, ignoring her, more interested in what her carer was doing on the other side of the room.

'Amelia, darling, come to Mummy.'

The baby turned her head, finally seeing her outstretched arms. To Victoria's horror her face crumpled and she shrank back, looking for comfort elsewhere. Blinded by tears she ran from the room. Her daughter had made the decision for her. However hard it was going to be, she had to leave. She had already lost her daughter. There was nothing to keep her here any more.

PART II

AFRICA AND INDIA, 1943–1944

10

FINAL FAREWELL

'You have four days' embarkation leave, Nurse Jones. You must follow the instructions you have been given to the letter. Good luck and congratulations on becoming a state registered nurse. You should be able to complete your training whilst on duty abroad.'

Victoria left the matron's office with mixed feelings. It would be relief to leave bomb-torn London and the constant stream of injured civilians who poured into the hospital every night. She was being posted somewhere overseas and was hoping it would be India. She longed to feel the warmth of the sun and inhale the intoxicating smell of her home.

'Nurse Jones, I understand you are leaving us today?' The grey-haired doctor held out his hand. 'I shall miss your happy smile and my patients will miss your competence.'

She offered her hand and it disappeared in a two-handed clasp. 'Thank you, Doctor Russell I have enjoyed my three years here. I don't think I could have had a better training anywhere else.'

'We do our best. It is a great shame so many of our staff feel the necessity to volunteer to serve overseas. Nevertheless I wish you *bon voyage*, my dear. When this wretched war is over I hope you will return to St Thomas's. Nurses of your calibre are hard to find.'

'That is kind of you to say so, sir. Now if you will excuse me, I have to catch a train in an hour.'

'Of course, of course. You have to say your final farewells to your family in Essex. Good luck, Nurse Jones.'

She watched the man who had been her inspiration walk away. Several times he had found her crying in the sluice room, on the point of handing in her notice. On each occasion he had taken her to his tiny cubbyhole office, made her a mug of tea and convinced her she had what it took to become an excellent nurse. She would never have completed her training, or done so well in her final exams, without his help.

She hurried through the hospital, eager to return to the nurses' home and change out of her uniform for the last time. Her instructions had been to report to an address in London in civvies. She presumed tropical kit would be issued then. Her destination was somewhere hot because she had endured several inoculations for various tropical diseases, which could only mean she was heading for Africa or India.

Having lived with the endemic diseases of her country without succumbing to them she had acquired a natural immunity, but in her second false persona as a childless, English widow she had been unable to tell them of her background.

* * *

Liverpool Street station was crowded and she was one of the few not in uniform. She hoped she would be allowed to board the train as service personnel always took precedence. She had rehearsed her reasons for needing to return to Brentwood and hoped if stopped it would be by a sympathetic guard.

Petrol for non-combatants was non-existent and she expected to be met by her mother-in-law with the pony trap. As usual there were no seats on the train and she prepared to jam herself into a corner between two grinning, khaki-clad young men.

'Budge up, Ron. Give the young lady some breathing space,' the taller of the two said cheerfully. Obediently his friend shuffled sideways leaving her just enough room to lean against the window. She didn't want to find herself stranded halfway down the narrow corridor as her stop was fifth and it could sometimes take two stops to fight her way back to the door.

'Thank you. I'm getting out at Brentwood and need to be this end.' Having travelled back and forth dozens of times over the past three years she was well used to balancing, her back pressed firmly to the glass, her small overnight bag tucked securely between her feet.

'I'm Fred Perkins, miss, and that's my mate Ron Jones. We're stationed at Colchester. Bin there bloomin' ages. About time us reserves were sent abroad to do our bit.'

She nodded sympathetically. She had heard this complaint several times from a variety of soldiers, all eager to get into combat like their compatriots in the air force and navy. 'I'm a nurse and this is my last leave before I get sent somewhere overseas.'

'Good for you, luv. I wish we was going with you.

All we do is march and practise with our guns. When I was called up last year I thought I would be in the thick of it by now.'

Ron punched his friend on the shoulder. 'Think yourself lucky, mate. We'll be fighting soon enough and then you'll be wishing yourself back in Blighty.'

The warmth of the September sun burning through the glass was becoming distinctly uncomfortable and she shifted so she was facing outwards and her back was resting on a compartment door. The train lurched to a second halt but few people alighted. 'How many stations is it to Brentwood, miss?' Tom asked as the train rattled off again.

'Usually it's the fifth, but I have to keep an eye out as sometimes the train misses out one of the stops. I've done this journey so often that I recognise the platforms now.' She smiled. 'It was different when they first removed the names. I stood with my nose pressed to the window all the way, terrified I would miss my stop.'

'Not married, then, miss?' Tom gestured with his head at her ringless left hand.

'No, footloose and fancy-free – that's me.' She was used to fielding personal questions of this nature from itinerant service personnel. Initially it had been difficult to respond to total strangers, but now she was happy to talk to whoever she was jammed up against. It was hard to remain aloof when you were sharing the same air as your neighbour.

The train bumped and rattled its way to Brentwood, arriving only ten minutes late. After saying goodbye to her companions, she squeezed her way to the exit grateful someone else had already alighted, leaving the door swinging open. Although she had mastered the intricacies of the leather strap and external handle, she had never forgotten her first attempt, which had left her swinging painfully over the platform.

Mr Hoskins, the ancient stationmaster, was obviously on his lunch break so she left her ticket on the windowsill by the exit gate.

'Victoria, my dear girl, perfect timing.' Marion called loudly from the dilapidated pony trap. 'I've only just arrived myself. Last time your train was almost an hour late so I thought I had bags of time.'

'It's so kind of you to meet me. I'm quite capable of walking a few miles to The Rookery, especially when it's such lovely weather.' Victoria ran across and scrambled into the cart and tossed her small bag onto the seat. She exchanged hugs with her mother-in-law. 'I have three days this leave, Marion, and I want to spend every minute with Amelia.'

'Of course you do, my dear. I have given Nanny the time off and she has gone to visit her sister in London. Amelia wanted to come with me, but we decided travelling in this contraption wouldn't be safe for an adventurous three-year-old.' Her mother-in-law made no comment about the extra day's leave. She was dreading telling her this was embarkation leave. When she had been asked if she was prepared to serve overseas, just before she took her final exams, she had agreed not realising her departure would be so soon after she qualified.

'I expect her grandpa is keeping her entertained.' Victoria gripped the wooden edge of the seat as Marion encouraged the pony into a spanking trot. 'How are you getting on with bicycle riding? Last time I was here you were determined to cycle everywhere.'

'Arthur has commandeered the bicycle. He's made a little seat for Amelia and he takes her out every day for a ride.' She smiled fondly. 'It is a delight to watch the two of them together. He was away when Henry was little and missed so much. Leaving Amelia in our care, my dear, has transformed our lives.'

'I know she's in the best possible place. It's only right she grow up where her father did.'

The journey to The Rookery was accomplished in record time. As the sweating pony skidded to a halt the front door swung open and a diminutive figure erupted from the entrance.

'Mummy! Mummy, I've been waiting and waiting for you to come.' Amelia, dark brown plaits flying, danced down the steps. Victoria bent, arms extended to receive her. She swung her around, inhaling the sweet scent of freshly washed child.

'Sweetheart, how you've grown. You're such a big girl now, and what a pretty dress you're wearing. Is it new?'

Amelia wriggled to get down. She was not a child who enjoyed cuddling. 'Grandma made it for me.' The little girl held out the pale yellow cotton skirt. 'She made it from an old dress. Do you like the bumpy bits at the top?'

Victoria stroked her daughter's head. 'I love them. It's called smocking, darling, and it would have taken Grandma ages to do. You're a very lucky girl to have such a pretty dress.' She waved to Arthur who was standing in the open doorway to greet her. She would like to have held her daughter's hand as they ascended the steps but she snatched it away and rushed ahead.

'Welcome, Victoria. You look tired, my dear. They

work you too hard at that hospital. How long are you staying? Do you have to be back on duty tomorrow?'

'No, I have an extra day. I'll tell you about it later on. I hope I'm not too late for lunch? I've not eaten since I came off duty this morning.'

'Good grief, Victoria! Have you been up all night? No wonder you look tired.' Marion bustled up behind her. 'Come along in, we have a lovely *al fresco* meal ready in the garden.'

The afternoon sped by and Amelia's bath time arrived too soon. Despite the fact she had been up for more than thirty-six hours Victoria was determined not to waste a moment of the precious time she had with her daughter.

When she had finished reading the obligatory bedtime story Amelia was still wide awake. 'Mummy, why are you yawning all the time? Is it your bedtime too?'

'I think it is, darling. Do you mind if I stretch out beside you for a moment? It's your turn to tell me a story now.'

When the dinner gong sounded Victoria was fast asleep next to her daughter and didn't hear it.

* * *

'Mummy? What are you doing in my bed? And you have your clothes on.'

Sleepily Victoria opened her eyes and kissed her child. 'Good morning, darling. Naughty Mummy fell fast asleep and never went away.' She sat up relieved to find someone had removed her shoes. 'I think it's morning, Amelia. Shall we open the blackout and see?'

She scrambled out of bed, amused to see the creases in her slacks. She turned to lift her daughter but the little girl avoided her grasp and wriggled to the floor unaided.

'Can I do the curtains, please, Mummy? Nanny never lets me.'

'Shall we do it together? We don't want to tear them, do we?'

The early-morning sunshine poured into the nursery, flooding it with light. 'What do you want to wear today, Amelia? Is your yellow dress still clean?'

'Nanny says I need clean clothes.'

'Well, that's fine. Shall we go and choose them? When you're dressed you can come and help me get ready.'

Victoria had only one change of clothes with her and these were no longer in her bag. 'My frock has disappeared, darling? Wherever can it be?' She pretended to search under the bed and behind the curtains.

'It's here, Mummy. I've found it. I've found it.'

'In the wardrobe! Now why didn't I think of that? What a clever girl you are.'

'Nanny says my daddy was very clever too. He could say lots of words, just like me.'

After three years the mention of Henry no longer caused her pain. She could hardly remember what he looked like and their short time together seemed like a distant dream. She was glad Amelia was living in her father's home surrounded by the people who had brought him up. She quickly stripped off her crumpled clothes and stepped naked into the bath where she had run an inch of water.

Her daughter was fascinated at the unusual sight of her mother without clothes on. 'Mummy, why do you have hairy bits down there?'

'Because I'm a grown-up woman, darling. When you're big you'll look just like this.'

Victoria reached over for the towel and quickly wrapped it round her. She could just imagine Nanny's face when Amelia asked her the same question. She felt a bubble of laughter and the thought of Arthur's reaction if her daughter asked him about his hairy bits. She should have been more discreet.

Keeping her back firmly to her child she scrambled into her clean underwear and hurried back into her room to grab the dress from the wardrobe.

'Come along, Amelia. I missed my dinner last night and my tummy is absolutely empty. Do you think Cook might have some eggs we could boil for breakfast?'

Chattering happily, the little girl bounced down the back stairs, completely unfazed by the lack of light. Arthur had removed every other light bulb from the stairway in an effort to conserve energy. There were no longer any inside staff, apart from the cook and the nanny; they had all left for more pressing war duties. Outside two geriatric gardeners and a simple stable boy looked after the grounds and pony.

She smiled as she recalled the shock she had received when she had come back for a visit to find half the park had been ploughed up and planted with potatoes and that the barn was full of chickens.

At least she was always sure of eating well when she came down to see her daughter. The kitchen door was open and she could hear Mrs Roberts talking to someone in the yard. Amelia was obviously outside as well. The table was laid for two and she was delighted to see a generous dish of butter in pride of place. The kettle on the range began to hiss and she walked over to move it to one side. She knew better than to interfere by making the tea herself.

Curious about the continued absence of the conscientious, elderly cook she wandered over to the door and stepped into the warm sun. Mrs Roberts turned from her conversation with Tommy, the least decrepit of the two outside men.

'Good morning, Mrs Hindley-Jones. Bert and I were talking about that dreadful business in Paris yesterday.'

'I'm sorry, Mrs Roberts, but I missed the nine o'clock news last night. What happened in Paris?'

The cook glanced around to check Amelia was out of earshot before answering. 'I expect you already know about that German minister being shot to death in broad daylight on the Etoile in Paris?'

'Yes, I was amazed the French Resistance could execute someone as important as Ritter so easily.'

'Well, the Nazis took fifty Frenchmen hostage and executed them as a reprisal. What a world we're living in! How much longer is this blooming war going to go on for?'

'Until Hitler is dead and the Germans are defeated. Now Italy has capitulated and Mussolini has fallen I'm sure it won't be long before our troops march into Germany.'

Bert removed his cap before speaking. 'Our boys are doing a grand job, but I doubts we could ever win the war without the Yanks over here to help us. They ain't popular with some folks with their big smiles and fat wallets, but if they hadn't come last year I reckon Hitler would be here by now.' The old man scratched his bald head before replacing his cap. 'Good to see you, missus; you're doing this family proud.'

'Thank you, Bert. We all have to do our bit and all the potatoes and vegetables you're growing are just as important.' She called her daughter and led her back into the kitchen where Mrs Roberts was busy boiling them an egg.

'Come and sit down, Amelia.' Victoria looked round for the towelling bib her daughter had worn last time she had visited. 'I can't find your bib. Do you know where it is?'

Amelia beamed. 'I don't need it any more. Nanny says I'm a big girl now and can eat my food without spilling it.'

'How wonderful! Are you going to tuck a napkin under your chin, like this? When I dip a soldier into an egg I often drip it all over the place.'

As soon as both napkins were firmly in place Mrs Roberts served breakfast. 'There are these first and then I thought you might like some hot toast and butter with damson jam. We still have coffee if you would prefer it?'

'No, thank you. Tea will be lovely. It tastes so much better here. I think it might be the difference in the water.'

The meal was almost finished when her father-in-law sauntered in. 'Good morning, what a lovely surprise. Both my favourite girls in the same room at the same time.'

'Grandpa, Grandpa; come and sit with me. I've had a egg and toast and I'm all full up.'

'How are you, Arthur? You look very well.'

'I'm in excellent health, thank you, Victoria my dear. And I must say you look a lot better than you did yesterday. Nothing like a good night's sleep and a hearty breakfast to put one right.' He pulled out a chair next to his granddaughter. 'Have you any plans for today? I know you like to spend as much time as possible with Amelia, but Marion and I thought you might like to go for a picnic.'

Before she could answer Amelia squealed with excitement. 'A picnic! Yes please, Grandpa. Can we go on your bicycle?'

'Well, darling, I don't think there's enough room for Mummy and Grandma on one bicycle. I rather thought we could take the pony and trap because we can all sit in that together.'

'Goody! Can I leave the table, Grandpa? I'm going to tell Grandma about the picnic.'

'Yes, off you go. Your grandma was in the study a few minutes ago.'

Victoria smiled sadly as she watched her daughter run off. The little girl didn't need her; she had her grandparents and Nanny to love and care for her. Each time she visited Amelia was less eager to see her, less bothered when she left. There was nothing she could do about it. It was how things were.

'I should love to go on a picnic, Arthur. I don't come down just to see Amelia, you know.'

'Didn't think you did, my dear. You've become an important part of our lives. Henry would be happy we all get on so well, don't you think?'

Her eyes filled. How was she going to tell these two, who had become so dear to her, that she was going overseas and would not see them again until the war was over?

Arthur, mistaking her tears, patted her on the shoulder. 'Now, Victoria. Henry would not want you to grieve for him any more. Time to get on with your own life now.'

'I have been doing so, haven't I? I don't wear a wedding ring and I'm known as Nurse Jones. I'm not sad because of Henry, it is something else. Something I haven't told you and Marion about.' She watched his expression change and thought he might have guessed what she was going to tell him. 'Shall I wait until Marion gets here or shall I tell you and leave you to explain to her?'

'Tell me. It's not good news. I'd rather hear it now than worry about it all day.'

'Some time ago I was asked if I would be prepared to serve overseas and I agreed. I didn't think anything would happen until I was fully trained and that won't be for another year. But I'm being called up now. This is my leave. When I go on Monday I won't be coming back until the war is over. I have no idea where I'm being sent, but I've had all the tropical jabs so it's Africa or India.'

'My dear girl, I don't know what to say. Africa? India? It hardly bears thinking of. At least there are not so many U-boats around to sink your ship.' He struggled clumsily to his feet, his face averted. 'Excuse me, something in my eye.'

Neither of them mentioned the worst part of this

scenario – the fact that by the time she was free to return to England her daughter would have forgotten who she was. Her throat closed and she swallowed hard, not wishing to give in to the tears that had been so near the surface ever since she'd been given her orders.

'Here, madam, drink this. Nothing like a cup of tea to cheer you up.' Mrs Roberts plonked a fresh cup in front of her. 'You're doing the right thing, if you'll forgive me for saying so. That little girl of yours has everything she needs right here. Our poor boys fighting for their lives amongst the heathens in India need you more.'

Victoria sipped her drink, the hot, sweet liquid gradually calming her, hardly hearing the cook's encouraging words. Tea was the panacea for all catastrophes. Death, birth and disaster – it would all make sense if you drank a cup of tea. When the content of Mrs Roberts's final sentence finally registered a wave of resentment swept over her.

Replacing her cup in the saucer with such force it slopped over the freshly scrubbed table, somehow she managed to restrain herself from answering the woman's unthinking, hurtful remark. How she wished she could say who she was. This was the one thing that made her imminent departure bearable.

She was possibly returning to her beloved India and might be able to contact her parents.

They didn't know Amelia had been born safely, didn't know Henry was dead or that she had just qualified as a nurse. Four years ago she had been the spoilt only child of a rajah, but look at her now. She was an independent, professional woman ready to face whatever fate had in store for her.

When she sailed away from England she was unlikely to return. However much it hurt, she must abandon her daughter. She couldn't take Amelia from her beloved grandparents – and she daren't risk telling them the truth about her background in case they rejected her daughter.

She hated the bombed and dreary country she was living in. She desperately craved the warmth and excitement of her home. When she said goodbye to Amelia and her in-laws it might well be for the last time, although she would not tell them of her decision until she wrote her final letter. The one that would not be posted until six weeks after she'd sailed away.

As soon as she had known she was leaving Britain she had been to see a solicitor. She had left copies of her birth and marriage certificates, the journal that she had been writing since she was seven years old and had continued religiously until Henry died. This would clarify everything. The letter she'd enclosed would explain the rest.

A letter for Amelia
England 1943

My darling daughter,

When you open this, on your 21st birthday, you will be a young woman and will not remember who I am. I'm certain you will be beautiful, intelligent and a loving, caring person, just like your dear father.

Inside the box you will find a journal. In it I have written the story of how your father and I met, but more importantly it explains who I am, and who you really are, and I hope it helps you to understand why I couldn't stay with you.

I hope you can understand, my darling Amelia, why we had to conceal my background. I hope one day you meet a man who will mean so much to you that you are prepared to give up everything for him. Your father and I had such a pitifully short time together, but every moment was perfect, every memory I have a sweet one.

Giving you up was even harder. When I decided to return to India as a nurse I couldn't take you away from your grandparents. You were their life; without their only son they had nothing else to live for. So for the second time I was forced to leave behind, forever, a part of my flesh. I shall always love you, and shall think of you every day of my life. If, after you read this, you want to find me, I shall be waiting, but will understand if you prefer not to. You can contact me through the solicitors who sent you this.

I hope that our letters, and the photographs and certificates, will explain everything.

Your devastated mother,
Victoria Hindley-Jones
Née Bahani

11

IN THE ARMY NOW

Victoria hardly noticed the tedious train journey from Brentwood to Liverpool Street, or her slow progress to King's Cross on the trolley bus. She moved like an automaton, not registering the noise and bustle; if she stopped to think about what she'd done – about never seeing her darling child again – she would be unable to function. In the letter, that would be posted to her in-laws after she left England, she had asked for regular reports of Amelia's progress, suggesting they communicate via the solicitor. This way she would be able to keep her anonymity but still have contact, however remote, with her daughter and the two people she'd come to love as much as her own parents.

The decision had been made weeks ago when she'd signed the forms and sent them to the Ministry of Defence. She was a member of the Queen Alexandra's Nursing Corps and must obey orders like any other member of the armed forces. Hers were to be at King's Cross station at midday; what happened next she had no idea, but as long as she didn't have to make the decisions she believed she would be able to cope with the blanket of misery that weighted her down.

The train was steaming gently, the porters eager to slam shut the doors and let the guard wave his green flag. She scrambled into the designated carriage and collapsed in the last available seat. Oblivious to the other occupants she closed her eyes and tried to hold back her tears.

Someone shook her none too gently by the shoulder. 'Sorry, but if you're QA you need to get your skates on.'

She opened her eyes and stared at the speaker. 'QA? I'm sorry, I don't understand.'

'Queen Alexandra nurse. Are you getting off at Hatfield with us?' The woman was ten years her senior and seemed irritated by Victoria's denseness. This was enough to snap her out of her lethargy.

'Obviously – I wouldn't be in this compartment if I wasn't.'

'In which case, I should grab your case and follow me. The train's stopping.' The woman vanished through the sliding door and it was only then Victoria realised she was alone. Frantically she grabbed her bag and, squeezing her way past the standing passengers, attempted to edge along the narrow corridor, praying the train wouldn't leave before she managed to get out.

A loud female voice shouted above the babble of conversation. 'Move over – damn you. Can't you see there's a nurse trying to get out?'

Immediately backs were flattened against the walls and Victoria found herself handed from person to person until she emerged, like a rat from a drainpipe, at the side of her rescuer.

'Thank you so much. I'm sorry I was rude just now – I was half asleep.'

'Not to worry. Come along – the whistle is about to be blown.'

Victoria leapt from the train, landing beside the woman who had been the only one to bother to wake her and make sure she got off when she should have. 'I'm Victoria Jones. If it wasn't for you I'd still be on there. Thank you once more.'

Her hand was grasped in a firm handshake. 'Dora Lancaster – pleased to meet you. You looked done in so we decided to let you sleep. I volunteered to wake you and make sure you got off in time.' Dora laughed, startling the pigeons pecking round their feet. 'Nearly made a mess of it too. Should have roused you sooner. Never mind – we're both off safe and sound.'

'Where's everyone else though? We appear to be the only two left on the platform.' She waited to be told what to do. Dora was obviously used to taking charge.

'Outside. Come along, my girl, quick march; don't want to be left to walk to Hatfield House do we?'

She certainly didn't and broke into a fast trot. Dora increased her pace and they ran down the concrete like two schoolgirls, their cases swinging wildly. They burst out of the station to find the other girls waiting quietly by the road.

She joined this group of nervous new recruits, red-faced and smiling. Their precipitous arrival released the tension. By the time the girls were directed into waiting ambulances and taken to Hatfield House, she felt more positive.

Dora sat next to her. 'Did you know they converted Hatfield House into a military hospital and it's also used as a mobilisation centre for bods like us, medical and nursing personnel?'

'I didn't even know I was being sent to Hatfield House until you told me a moment ago. All I knew was that I had to be at King's Cross by midday today.'

'Good God!' Dora shouted down the ambulance. 'How many of you lot knew where you were going?' Her stentorian tones ricocheted round the vehicle and six heads shot round. One by one the girls admitted they had had no idea where they were going either. Dora nodded. 'Thought so. Only senior staff have been told. Bloody ridiculous! Still, what do you expect when things are run by a group of old men?'

Having started the conversation soon everyone was chipping in with names and home towns. All, apart from Dora, were newly qualified, and this would be their first real nursing post. Victoria began to feel the numbness dissipate under the barrage of questions and concern given by her new colleagues. They wrapped her in a blanket of kindness, which almost made her loss bearable. No one asked what she'd had to leave behind – her grief must be written on her face.

The bumpy ride ended abruptly, sending three of the occupants into a heap on the floor amidst much swearing and giggling. She joined the line of girls threading their way in through the impressive front door and was sorry to see Dora stride off in a different direction. Presumably to join the other matrons and sisters in a different part of the vast, old-fashioned building.

She stood behind a girl wearing a green felt hat that entirely covered her hair. The young woman stepped back, treading on her toe.

'I'm sorry; did I tread on your foot? Oh bugger! Look, I've made a hole in your stocking. I'm sorry.' The speaker, a young woman about her own age, with sparkling green eyes, turned as she apologised and Victoria understood why the hat was pulled down so firmly. The flaming red hair hidden beneath it would have stopped the traffic even on a dull day.

'That's all right. I don't suppose we'll be wearing these civilian things for much longer anyway.' Victoria held out her hand. 'I'm Victoria Jones. I've just taken my state finals. What about you?'

The girl grinned showing a row of gappy teeth. 'I'm Molly Smith. I trained in Chesterfield and I took my exams last month as well. Any idea what happens next?'

She looked around the busy room filled with others like themselves, all in civilian clothes clutching a small suitcase and waiting to be told what to do.

'I haven't a clue. But somebody did tell me all nurses are made into the equivalent of lieutenants. That means we'll be officers in the British Army. I must say I don't feel much like an officer – I'm scared witless.'

Molly squeezed her arm sympathetically. 'Blimey! Fancy that. My brothers are all privates in the army. Do you think they'll have to salute me if we meet?' The girl grinned. 'It'll make a change from a clip round the ear, that's for sure.'

She was about to answer when a senior matron from the War Office appeared in the doorway and the room fell silent.

'Good afternoon; you will be at Hatfield House until you get the order to leave. That could be several weeks. Until then you will occupy yourself in the wards of this hospital. Your uniforms will be issued in turn. You must also learn to march and to salute. When you have your embarkation orders you will be reissued with the correct equipment for your destination. Now follow me.'

Victoria and her new friend fell in together and the twenty girls half marched, half shuffled behind the formidable lady to start their new lives.

* * *

Victoria and Molly discovered they were billeted in a civilian house about a mile away. The four other girls who were to share the billet seemed a sociable lot and she thought they would soon settle in together. She had been used to working and sleeping with other women and was quite happy to continue to do so.

Their landlady, Mrs Frobisher, welcomed them warmly. 'Come along, my dears, I'll show you where you're sleeping. It's up in the attic, but in spite of that it's nice and snug. There are two dormer windows that open and good, thick blackout curtains to cover them and also keep out the cold winds.'

She puffed off in front of them, unable to speak whilst climbing the narrow, creaky staircase. Breathlessly she paused on the small landing and pointed into the long room the girls were to occupy during their stay in Hatfield.

'There you are. You have a bed each – no sharing here. And the ceiling's too low for bunks so you're all on the basement. There's a chest of drawers between two of you, and two wardrobes to share.' The middle-aged lady pointed at the single suitcase each carried. 'Not that you've much to hang up at the moment. But just you wait and see; by the time you've got all the bits and pieces you'll need to take away with you those wardrobes will be bursting.'

Victoria led the others into the room. She looked around, pleased with the neat row of matching iron bedsteads all covered with candlewick counterpanes. 'It's lovely, Mrs Frobisher. I'm sure we'll all be very happy here. I expect it will be sunny in the morning. Considering it's December, and the temperature must be almost freezing outside, it's really warm in this room.'

'That's because there's two chimneys run up through here, one from the kitchen range, which is on all the time, and the other from the big fire in the parlour. When I've got guests I always keep that alight as well. Here, put a hand on this, and you'll see what I mean.'

One of the girls – a tall, thin blonde – walked over and leant against the chimney breast. She spoke with a crystal-clear, upper-class accent. 'You are so right. It is lovely and warm. This isn't nearly as bad as I expected; in fact it's a lot more acceptable than the nurses' home I have been living in for the last three years. It reminds me of Snow White's cottage, but we have only six beds in here.'

The landlady left them to settle in and each girl

selected her bed and unpacked her meagre belongings.

'The matron said we had this evening to settle in
and read the rule book. Do you think we have to stay
up here and do it, or will we be allowed to use the
sitting room?'

Victoria thought for a moment. 'I don't know,
Molly, but Mrs Frobisher seems a friendly sort. We
can ask what she wants us to do when we have supper. Anyone any idea when that is, by the way?'

Angela, the blonde, wandered over to a piece of
paper pinned tidily to the front of one of the
wardrobes. 'I say, this has all the things we need to
know written on it. Jolly good! Food will be served at
five o'clock and it also says that we get cocoa and biscuits at nine thirty before we retire.'

Jenny, a petite brunette, curled up already on her
chosen bed, called over. 'Sounds just like a nurses'
home. What time are lights out and is there a curfew
set? But far more importantly, when do we get to have
our weekly bath?'

Angela continued reading. 'It says if we require a
front door key we have to ask: breakfast is at six
thirty. Ye gods! That means an early start.' She
quickly scanned the sheet. 'Ah! Yes – here we are. The
bathroom is on the floor below, as is the lavatory, and

we can use the facilities any time between six and nine thirty.'

Victoria finished arranging her hairbrush and bits and pieces on the shared bedside table. 'I expect we have to be on the ward by seven thirty and it's a mile to walk. That's if we're on days, of course, but I'm not sure how it will work here, or how much nursing we will actually do. I think, from what Matron said in her talk earlier, we're really only here long enough to equip us and train us for military life.'

Molly chuckled. 'Military life? It can't be any worse than living-in where I did and working in the infirmary. I tell you, my matron was worse than any sergeant major.'

There was still an hour to go before supper and they spent it getting to know each other and explaining a little about their backgrounds and why they had decided to join up. Once again Victoria was forced to offer half-truths. She told them she had been widowed at Dunkirk, that her parents were dead and that she had been living with her in-laws until she started her nurse training three years before.

She made no mention of Amelia or India. As far as everyone was concerned she was an independent Englishwoman with no ties of any sort, exactly the sort of young person the War Office wanted in the Queen Alexandra's. Not being able to talk about her darling daughter was breaking her heart. Every minute that passed she regretted her decision and wished the letter to her in-laws unwritten.

When they clattered downstairs later, Victoria sat next to Molly at the large oak dining room table, but she had little appetite.

'It's a bonus that there's an inside lav on the first floor, and a bathroom with hot and cold running water. Mind you, the geyser looks a bit antiquated. Bags it's not me who has to use it first,' Molly said cheerfully.

'And there's a black Plimsoll line painted around the tub to make sure we don't use more than our allotted inches,' Angela informed the rest of the table.

'Thank God for that! I had visions of using a pot and then having to trek down the garden to empty it every morning,' Jenny said with considerable relief.

Victoria offered to help Mrs Frobisher serve. Hiding her distress was becoming increasingly difficult.

'No, my dear, you stay in the dining room with the others. It's my pleasure, looking after you nurses. I'm just doing my bit for the war effort. It's you girls who

are going overseas to look after all our brave servicemen.'

'In that case, I shall go and sit down again. I must
say something smells delicious.'

A few minutes later the dining room door swung
open and a thinner version of their landlady appeared carrying a large tray with six steaming bowls
of leek and potato soup.

'Here you are, my dears. My sister says there's
plenty more if you want seconds. Good country cooking, that's what you'll get here, so make the most of it.
You'll not get anything decent to eat when you leave
these shores.'

The aromatic soup was followed by a tasty vegetable pie with jacket potatoes and they even had
stewed apple and custard for dessert. Victoria's appetite returned – it seemed churlish not to enjoy the
food when Mrs Frobisher had taken the trouble to
prepare it.

'I'm stuffed full,' Molly said happily, rubbing her
distended stomach. 'I don't think I've eaten so much
since last Christmas. Blimey, if we get fed like this
every day I'll be as fat as a pig before we go and none
of my new uniform will fit me.'

Victoria looked around the table. 'None of us are
exactly overweight, are we? Running around the

wards for three years on the rations we've been getting has made us thin. It won't do us any harm to stock up for a few weeks.'

'Are you always so practical, Victoria?' Angela enquired, raising her perfectly plucked eyebrows.

'I'm afraid so, yes. It helps to be practical in our profession, don't you think?'

There was a general chorus of assent. Despite her upper-crust manners Angela Dewberry had to be as hard-working, intelligent and practical as the rest of them in order to have completed her final examinations successfully. They were equal now, all junior lieutenants in the British Army. She wondered what her parents might think of their daughter scrubbing out bedpans and cleaning up vomit for a living. Thinking about seeing them again one day helped alleviate her misery.

12

EQUIPMENT AND EMBARKATION

Victoria woke early knowing if she didn't get up to use the facilities before everyone else she might not get her turn at all. She slipped out of the attic and had a quick 'wash up and wash down' as she'd come to call it. She scampered back, teeth chattering; the temperature had dropped dramatically overnight and the stairs and landings were unheated.

'Molly, you go next – no one else's awake yet.' Victoria shook her new friend vigorously and the girl groaned, rolled over and opened one cautious eye.

'God, you're keen. What's the time?'

'It's five forty-five and the water's hot. I heard someone downstairs getting breakfast ready. And it looks like it's going to snow.'

'Well, I'm awake now, so I might as well get up. I wish we'd been issued with a QA's uniform. I rather fancied myself in scarlet and grey.'

'We'll have to do with whatever they give us. I think we get khaki like the rest of the army.' Victoria dressed quickly in the clothes she'd arrived in yesterday. She had a warm, woollen skirt, thick lisle stockings and a long-sleeved flannelette blouse. The violently striped hand-knitted jumper had been a parting present from Marion.

Sounds of the other girls waking prompted Molly to jump out of bed, grab her dressing gown, ram her feet into her dilapidated slippers and run down the stairs. There was only one lavatory and it was going to be in demand at any moment.

Breakfast was porridge served with top of the milk and a sprinkling of sugar. Not Victoria's favourite start to the day, but it was warm and filling.

'I wonder if we get toast as well?' Jenny asked.

Angela sniffed elegantly. 'I think I can smell some coming. I can't believe I'm hungry after all we ate last night. We're going to need to stoke up. It's freezing and sleeting outside and it's still pitch-dark. I'm certainly not looking forward to the walk to the hospital.'

At seven o'clock they were ready – hats, coats and

gloves on. Although officially sunrise, there was no sign of light; outside was still a gloomy grey.

'We're going to need our torches. I had a bloomin' hard job getting any batteries this time. I hope the army has a decent supply. It's a good thing it's a direct route; you can hardly see your hand in front of your face,' Molly grumbled as they set off.

Victoria tied her scarf more firmly, glad she'd had the foresight to put two hatpins into her beret. The December wind was icy and decidedly unpleasant. Her warm winter coat flapped uncomfortably around her knees as she trudged after Angela, one arm linked through Molly's, as much for reassurance as support.

They arrived bedraggled and barely five minutes before the stated time. They hurried to the large room they'd assembled in on arrival to find it already occupied by most of the girls. Victoria glanced around hoping to see her friend Joan, but she wasn't there.

'At least it's warm in here. The others have hung their things over the chairs. Shall we do the same?' Molly asked.

By the time the rest of their contingent arrived there was a strong smell of wet clothes as their outer garments gently steamed against the radiators. Not all the girls had been as fortunate as Victoria and her group; six were billeted in Hatfield House itself and spoke of the horrors of a bathtub hidden under a window seat with a lid like a coffin. No one had dared to use it in case they were trapped inside. It might have been built that way so it wouldn't spoil the ancient interior.

At seven forty-five the door at the far end swung open and Matron marched in, followed by a middle-aged man in army khaki and the insignia of a sergeant major. Victoria automatically straightened and stood approximately to attention.

'Good morning, ladies. This morning you will be issued with your drabs and when you're in uniform you will be directed to the drill hall where Sergeant Major will instruct you in saluting and marching correctly. After that you will return here and be allocated your ward duties.'

Victoria joined the queue at the quartermaster's stores to receive a cumbersome brown paper parcel, which weighed a ton. The girls had been given orders to go back to their billet and change, then report to the drill hall. They had two hours in which to accomplish their transformation from civilian nurse to army recruit.

Molly pressed her face up to the steamy window.

'Blimey! It's snowing out there and we've got to trudge a mile in either direction just to change. I'm going to find somewhere to do it here. Are you on, Victoria?'

Victoria was tempted to agree. 'Sounds like a good idea, Molly, but what are we going to do with our other clothes? We can't go to the drill hall with those under our arms; sadly I don't think we've got a choice. We'll have to go back.'

Clutching their brown paper parcels by the hairy string the girls began the long walk back to their temporary home. The wind was behind them and they almost ran the mile, arriving hot and covered with snow.

'I hope we can get back in at this time of day. Mrs F won't be expecting us,' Molly said as Angela raised her hand to bang on the front door.

Their landlady was a trifle flummoxed but soon recovered. 'Welcome, ladies, have you come back to change? If you hurry I'll have a nice mug of tea and freshly baked rock cakes waiting in the dining room when you come down.' Angela thanked her and they were trooping upstairs when she called after them. 'Hang your wet things on the pegs. That's what they're there for.'

Victoria looked for the promised pegs and saw three neatly arranged along each of the chimney breasts. The obvious place for drying wet garments. She removed her English civilian clothes for what might be the very last time and hung them on her allocated peg.

The sound of crackling brown paper filled the attic as the parcels were unwrapped. It was unlikely the clothes would be a good fit, but she hoped at least the army-issue knickers and bra would fit her. The khaki battledress had not been made to measure, as was usual with the scarlet and grey of the peacetime uniform of the Queen Alexandra's. The slacks and blouse had been allocated according to the measurements the girls had supplied on their initial application forms.

She found her slacks were a trifle large, but the sturdy leather belt that accompanied them took care of the problem. Her shirt was a good fit and the battledress was roomy, but not as big as the things Molly had been given.

'God help me! Look at this, Victoria. My shirt's long enough to wear as a nightie and the slacks are six inches too long.' Molly held up the slacks and the cuffs trailed below her feet. She looked round the room hopefully. 'Angela, you're the tallest, did you get the right size or do you want to swap with me?'

Angela held up her slacks and sure enough they were several inches too short. 'I think they must have given us the wrong parcels. Here, Molly, catch this.' The air was filled with flying clothes as amidst much hilarity the girls exchanged clothes, even down to the serviceable underwear.

By the time they were all dressed and ready they had fifteen minutes left to drink the promised tea.

'These greatcoats weigh a ton. If we're being sent to Africa or India, why on earth have they issued us with winter uniform?'

'Molly, use your noggin. We're going to be here for a few weeks; we've got to have something suitable to wear. It's December; we would freeze in tropical gear.'

Molly grinned and aimed a pretending punch at her. 'All right, clever clogs. Let's get downstairs. I can smell freshly baked something or others. Believe it or not, I'm hungry again. It seems a long time since we had breakfast.'

Fortified by rock cakes, whose main ingredient appeared to be carrots, but were delicious none-theless, and steaming mugs of hot tea, the girls donned their heavy topcoats and prepared to go out into the snow. With their collars turned up they emerged to do battle with the elements.

The return journey took longer as they were walking directly into the sleet and snow. Victoria wished they'd issued her with a hat as well. She wore her hair short and it was plastered to her skull and dripping unpleasantly down her neck when they eventually reached the sanctuary of the hall.

Inside the room was transformed. Instead of the gaggle of motley dressed young women there was now a platoon of khaki-clad female soldiers. Victoria stared around in amazement. What a difference a uniform made. It was hard to tell one nurse from the other and she was glad they had been divided into groups of six before the transformation had taken place.

Her group had been the last to arrive and only a few minutes later the RSM appeared. The squad automatically snapped to attention and waited for orders. He looked round the hall and his expression showed he was displeased. Victoria glanced nervously from side to side wondering in what way they had offended.

'Where are your bloody hats? You can't salute without a bloody hat,' he roared.

The lines of girls instinctively patted the vacant

spaces on their heads. They hadn't been issued with hats. Who was going to tell this fearsome man?

Angela raised her hand politely. 'Excuse me, sir, but hats were not issued to us this morning.'

Victoria watched the man swell. His florid cheeks expanded and his waxed moustache bristled with indignation. She braced herself for a barrage of abuse, but the man sighed noisily.

'Very well, ladies, we shall have to make do. Follow me. Quick march.'

She fell in behind the others and they were led through the driving snow to an unheated drill hall, and were all grateful for their heavy coats as they stood shivering, awaiting the promised headgear. Twenty minutes after their arrival the RSM returned, followed by two privates carrying cardboard boxes.

'Right, ladies. Fall in and get your bloody hats. Move yourselves. On the double.'

Inside the boxes Victoria saw a random collection of military hats, some appearing to date back to the Crimea. She was handed a First World War tin hat, which balanced on her head like a fruit bowl. She was convinced it would fly off if she had to move too fast.

Molly received a large Boer War slouch hat, Angela another tin hat and Jenny's looked like a pith helmet. Barbara and Mary, the other two from her billet, got scruffy forage caps. They put these on, trying to stifle their giggles and ignore the ominous muttering from their tormentor.

Suitably dressed she shuffled into her place in one of the straight lines and waited for the instruction to begin. She learnt to march in time and salute correctly, '*long way up – short way down*,' would be forever etched on her brain.

'Long way up – short way down,' the man screamed time and again until everyone eventually achieved it to his satisfaction. Then she was forced to stomp round and round the hall listening and responding instantly to the shouts of the instructor.

'Left, right, left, right, pick up your bloody feet. You're in the bloody army now. Eyes left, salute. Eyes right, salute. Don't roll your eyes about. You're not on the stage; you're in the bloody army.'

After an hour of this she no longer felt the urge to laugh and was glad she had been ordered to remove her coat when the drilling started. She was sweating, and her feet hurt where her new boots pinched unmercifully.

'Right, left, halt. Eyes right. Salute. Quick march. Left – right. Left – eyes left, salute.'

Victoria was responding automatically. She

stared ahead, not seeing anything, simply reacting to the commands. She just wanted this torture to end. After endless marching and saluting the ogre on the podium screamed at them for the final time.

'Squad, halt. At ease. Dismissed. Fall out.'

With sighs and groans of relief the girls fell out and the hated hats were thrown, with considerable force, back into the boxes. Greatcoats were recovered and shrugged into.

'What now? I'm bloody knackered.' Molly leant against the wall with her eyes closed. 'I could do with a fag. Anyone got one?'

'I didn't know you smoked, Molly?' Victoria said.

'I don't, well I don't very often, but just now I really want one. And a pint of beer would go down a treat as well.' Amidst general laughter the girls agreed that a cigarette and a pint of beer was exactly what they all needed. They agreed that when the weather improved they would go on a recce to find the nearest pub.

'It's two o'clock. Do you think we're going to get any lunch, Angela?' Jenny asked hopefully.

Angela buttoned up her coat. 'I should damn well hope so. Good God! They can't expect us to march up and down for hours and then not feed us.'

Victoria pulled her coat around her, sliding down

the wall until she was seated, knees under her chin and her arms curled round them. 'Well, I'm not going off to look for any. I'm staying right here until someone comes and tells me what to do next. Do you realise, Molly, we've walked four miles in the snow, and I should think another four miles in here.'

Molly collapsed beside her. 'Feels more like thirty miles. Mind you, I bet we walked a lot more when we were on the ward.'

One by one the girls followed Victoria's example and settled down to wait until their unelected leader returned with information about the missing meal.

* * *

The weeks passed and Christmas loomed. None of their draft had leave so that was one problem solved, as Victoria had nowhere to go. Keeping busy was the only way she could forget what she'd given up. She had to adjust or she wouldn't survive. She, like everyone else, made the best of it, singing carols and serving patients with the jolliest of smiles. For the first time since the war began, she heard church bells ringing out to celebrate the birth of Christ.

The wireless was turned up in the ward so everyone could listen to the king's speech at three.

After the national anthem had been played, Molly helped Victoria carry the radio back to its more usual resting place, in her office.

'Don't you think, Victoria, that His Majesty sounded a lot more cheerful this year? I suppose as there's less bombing and Italy has given up, things do look more hopeful.'

'But Germany is still fighting and things are as bad as ever in the Far East. Let's pray this is the last Christmas we spend at war.'

'Amen to that,' Molly said grinning. 'Come on, let's get things tidied up in there. We finish in an hour and Mrs F has promised us a real Christmas feast tonight.'

* * *

The New Year dawned and after the obligatory morning roll call Victoria rushed, as usual, to scan the mess noticeboard. When would news of their draft appear? Why was it always some other squad who was leaving? She wrote every week as promised to Marion and Arthur and enclosed drawings and encouraging words for her daughter. Each time she sealed the envelope it tore her apart. She ached to hold her darling child in her arms just once more, but knew this would never happen.

Eventually one morning in February she scanned the board and saw that the names of their draft were up. She turned to Molly, who was standing by her side. 'At last. It's our turn now. It says here we have to report to a depot in West London tomorrow. I wonder what that's all about.'

'I expect we have to be issued with some sort of special kit. At least we're no longer obliged to work on the wards and I think we'll get a three-day embarkation leave as well. Are you going to go back and see the in-laws?'

She shook her head. 'I've said goodbye. That part of my life is over and done with; they need to forget about their son and so do I. I shall stay here and enjoy having the attic to myself.' If Molly had known about Amelia she would have been horrified and thought her callous. So many lies – so much deceit.

The following morning they duly reported to the depot and were handed a bush hat each. Victoria knew where they were going – it had to be Africa. Clutching their hats the girls returned to Hatfield House where they were issued with a list of extra equipment the quartermaster's stores didn't stock.

They tried every shop in St Albans and Hatfield with no luck. Angela came up with a solution.

'We'll have to try London. If we divide into pairs and look for a couple of items each we shall find them much quicker than by traipsing around in a group.'

Victoria and Molly were designated to buy the flat irons and tent post straps, Angela and Jenny were looking for oil stoves and kettles, and Barbara and Mary the hurricane lamps. Within a few days they managed to procure the required items and their kit was complete.

The expected leave came and Molly opted to stay behind with Victoria. 'I'm not going to leave my best friend alone. We can spend the time in the pub and enjoying a bath whenever we want.'

Victoria's eyes were damp. 'That's so kind of you, Molly. To tell you the truth I was rather dreading rattling around up here on my own. I'm so used to being surrounded by people, being on my own would seem strange.'

The girls returned subdued from their home visits and this feeling of depression wasn't helped by the sixpenny will forms they were all handed at the first morning roll call.

'Blimey! This is a bit rich. Fancy asking us to write a will – talk about rubbing our nose in it.'

'It makes perfect sense, Molly. If we get killed someone has to inherit our back pay,' Victoria told her, laughing. Inside she was panicking – to whom could she write her will? Quickly she scribbled Molly's name and address and shoved it into the envelope before anyone could ask what she'd written. The army was in control of not only her life but also her death.

Once the luggage was packed and corded this was transported from the attic to a storeroom at Hatfield House. All they had left was their full winter kit, a change of underwear, night things and washbag.

She was the only one in the group actually looking forward to departure. No one else had travelled any distance, although Angela had gone to the continent before the war. This period of calm came to an abrupt end after an evening roll call when their draft was told to report back at 2100 hours wearing full kit and carrying an overnight bag with things for their journey.

As they got ready after supper on the final night Angela reminded them what Matron had said. 'We're supposed to tell Mrs Frobisher we're going for a walk. For heaven's sake, who's going to go out in the middle of the night in the blackout, wearing an overcoat over their outdoor uniform and a gas mask and tin hat draped around their neck?'

'Of course Mrs Frobisher won't believe it, but I expect it's happened several times before. She told us she always has nurses staying here and they all get sent overseas eventually.'

'Ever the practical one, Victoria – we can always rely on your common sense.'

She wasn't sure if Mary's comment was complimentary or not, but in the flurry of handing in her final letter she didn't have time to worry about it. Victoria watched the VAD walk away with hers. In it she had told Marion and Arthur that she was handing over her daughter's welfare and upbringing to them. She had written that it wasn't because she didn't love them, but was because she loved them too much.

At least they could still correspond via her lawyers in London. She wished for the umpteenth time she could tell them the truth. That it wouldn't be fair to take Amelia away from them and remove her to India, which was where she intended to live when the war finally ended. It was almost a relief to see the letter go. She had made the right decision, and maybe one day her beautiful daughter would come to understand why she had been abandoned in her infancy.

When the girls left the house it was strangely quiet, no lights on anywhere downstairs. She guessed their landladies, knowing what was come coming, had taken themselves off for the evening to avoid any possible embarrassment.

'Right, girls, are we ready? Onward and upward.' Angela, as always, took the lead with Jenny beside her. Victoria and Molly brought up the rear.

'I've lost count of the number of times we've made this journey. Doesn't it feel strange to know we'll never walk this particular way again?'

'Bloody good job, in my opinion. Nothing ever happens in the country – give me the city every time.'

It was too cold and strenuous to walk and talk so they completed their final journey from the billet to Hatfield House in companionable silence.

The other girls, those who lived in, told them they'd been served with a magnificent steamed treacle pudding for afters that night and there were choruses of envy from the twelve who had been billeted in civilian houses. They'd eaten well, but no one had had a treacle pudding.

Initially, as they squatted on the floor, the girls chatted and laughed, but as time dragged by slowly the room fell silent. A little after midnight the assistant matron returned and told them they were to leave.

'Now, I shall let you out in pairs. You mustn't speak, and don't drop anything. Good luck, ladies, and God speed.'

Victoria hissed to Molly, 'It's like the animals in the ark, two by two, into the unknown.' She stumbled after the others, downhill in the pitch-black, her tin hat clanking noisily against her gas mask. She was directed by a series of hidden speakers until she finally arrived at Hatfield station. Even in full kit her teeth were chattering, partly due to the cold but mostly from fear.

Eventually a long, dark train steamed into the station and almost invisible guards escorted them into an empty carriage. Automatically they divided into their accustomed groups and each six occupied a compartment. The train clanked and jerked, stopped and started, through a long weary night and half the next day.

Sometimes she slept fitfully, but others she joined in with the singing, but eventually the novelty wore off and the journey became tedious beyond measure. Hungry, tired and almost speechless from singing, Victoria stumbled out onto a bustling dockside upon which dozens of other girls milled about waiting to be directed somewhere else.

'Good God, we're in Scotland.'

'How do you know that?' Jenny asked her friend.

'I recognise this. It's Greenock and that water over there is the Clyde.'

Victoria followed Angela's pointing fingers and saw two aircraft carriers, battleships, corvettes and two other large vessels, anchored out to sea.

'I wonder which one is ours? It has to be one of those anchored next to the warships. Come along, girls, everyone's moving off now.'

'I hope we get something to eat soon, Angela, I'm starving,' Jenny wailed plaintively. Like everyone else the small thermos of tea and slim packet of sandwiches had not lasted long.

'For someone so small, you have a prodigious appetite. I can't imagine why you're so petite,' Angela told her friend severely.

Victoria resigned herself to another long wait, but surprisingly soon a group of sailors appeared and ushered them down to a light ship, which was to take them out to the *Stratheden*, the vessel they were to sail in.

Although she had travelled across the world she had done so in an aeroplane. This was her first time on board an ocean-going ship. She looked around with interest, and saw scrubbed deck and grey-painted railings everywhere. She was more cheerful now a weak winter sun was shining and they'd just been told an early supper would be served as soon as they got themselves settled in.

Angela appeared at her side. 'Wake up, Victoria – no time for daydreaming. I've commandeered an empty cabin. It has six berths and Jenny's holding it for us.'

She shook herself awake and with Molly close behind followed Angela down into the bowels of the ship to the small room that was to be her home for the next few days.

This cabin had once been a four berth but had been transformed to accommodate six by the addition of two extra bunks. These were arranged along three sides of the cabin. On the fourth wall was a large cupboard and washbasin. The narrow space between the berths was just wide enough for one person to stand sideways.

'Good God, it's going to be like playing sardines in here. I hope we don't have to do more than sleep in the cabin.' She had spoken without thinking and was merely stating the obvious.

'It won't be so bad. At least we're all together. It

would be horrible having to share with strangers, wouldn't it?'

Victoria smiled at Molly, grateful for her support. 'You're right of course. Stupid of me to complain – after all there's a war on, isn't there?'

13

AFRICA AT LAST!

That evening Victoria and Molly were the only two to venture outside. It was black, but they were not allowed to light a cigarette or flash a torch in case they were seen by a German U-boat or spotter plane.

'It's strange to think there are a dozen or so ships all within hailing distance of us and we can't see any of them.'

'Let's go back down, Victoria. It's perishing out here and I've barked my shins twice on some bloody sharp things sticking out.'

They turned to grope their way back down, relieved when they turned into a lit part of the narrow passage. They met several of their draft passing to and fro on their way from the canteen to their cabins, but didn't stop for a gossip.

'I think we should be around this next corner. Yes, here we are, Molly; this is us.' She had forgotten her initial disquiet about being incarcerated in their tiny cabin in their leisure time. The ship was packed to the gunwales, not a spare inch of space, and most of the occupants were male. She'd been told by their friendly steward that there were a contingent of WAAFs on board but she hadn't seen them so far. The only place they could be at night was in their cabin, for the canteen was available to them for meals and lectures only.

'Ah! The wanderers return,' Angela called out on their entrance. 'We were going to send out a search party if you didn't come back soon. What on earth were you doing up there in the dark?'

Victoria pulled off her greatcoat and carefully stowed it under her bunk. 'I should have listened to you, Angela – there's no point in going anywhere after dark. I shall have to get used to spending my evenings in here with you lot.'

'What's wrong with us then?' Mary said, propping herself up on her elbows.

'Nothing at all, it's just that I have a horror of

small spaces and down here in the bowels of the ship we don't even have a porthole to look out of.'

'You know, the *Lusitania* sank because people had left the portholes open. I'm glad we don't have one to worry about – one of the soldiers told me,' Mary said.

She settled down on her bunk and Molly scrambled into the one above her. The evening passed pleasantly enough. She listened to the girls telling anecdotes of their past and although she remained silent no one remarked on it. At nine o'clock their friendly steward appeared with a tray of tea.

'Here you are, ladies. I'm afraid there's no biscuits, but I expect one of you has some hidden away somewhere.'

She had two packets, bought in London with the last of her rations and handed them to Angela for distribution. 'I've been saving these. If we only have two each they should last us a few days.'

'Do you know how long we're going to be on this ship, Angela?' Molly asked.

'No idea, but if we're going to Africa we will have to go round Gibraltar, and that's a long way away. I expect it's going to be more than a few days, more like a few weeks before we arrive wherever we're going. I suppose we'd better get used to it.'

'We have to report on deck for the issue of lifejackets.' Jenny read from the list sent down with the tea. 'I think that must mean we will be sailing at first light; otherwise they would have given them to us when we arrived, wouldn't they?'

* * *

The following morning, after being fortified by a substantial breakfast, Victoria was issued with a life-jacket in the canteen. A sailor insisted on fitting it on for her.

'There you are, love. Make sure you pull it down hard and check the six straps are fastened the way I just showed you. If you get it wrong you'll float the wrong way up and drown. See, you've got a red torch on one shoulder and rations wrapped up in water-proof dangling from your other one.'

The young man leant across and clicked the light on and off. 'Good, that's working. Don't mess about with it – it's only if you fall in the water and then only at night.'

She mumbled her thanks and prayed she would never have to discover whether her battery had run out. The draft gathered with the rest of yesterday's newcomers to hear a lecture on emergency procedures.

'If you hear the buzzer you must go straight up on deck through the nearest exit. Wear your overcoat, hats, lifejacket and carry a water bottle. Remember to keep those filled always.'

Angela immediately raised her hand. 'Excuse me, but won't a greatcoat weigh you down in the water and be extremely heavy?'

The man grinned, obviously used to such questions. 'It's bloody cold on a lifeboat, miss, and I reckon many people would be alive today if they'd remembered to wear their greatcoats. Now, where was I? Yes, if there's a continuous ringing of bells and the buzzer, wear your tin hat. Remember to look after your torch and the rations because you have to hand them in at the end of the voyage.' This last remark was greeted by a chorus of laughter.

The young officer left and the tannoy system crackled and groaned into life. It repeated everything they'd just been told far more forcefully and with an extra proviso. 'Lifejackets must be carried at all times, day and night. To appear without one is a crime. Women services please note: if one of them is caught in an emergency without a jacket some damn fool of a man will give her his, and men are far more important in this war.'

After this last comment the loudspeaker grumbled into silence. 'Well, what a blooming cheek!' Molly was disgusted.

'Whoever he was, he doesn't like women on board,' Victoria answered crisply. 'But, he's quite right, isn't he? What do they say, women and children first? I should hate to put any man in the position of having to sacrifice his life to save mine.'

'And so says the gospel of Victoria,' Angela said wryly.

No sooner had the sailor vanished than the Tannoy stopped and the buzzer sounded.

'Come on, come on, girls, this is obviously a drill. We'd better get on deck and make sure we do everything right. We don't want to let the QAs down.'

'No, Lieutenant Dewberry, we don't,' Victoria said, saluting smartly. Although she quite liked Angela, there was definite friction between them. On deck she saw the passengers were packed into five lines and each of these had then been divided into sections. Their section was directed, not to a boat but to a rope as thick as a man's arm that hung limply over the side.

'Bloody hell! I hope we're not expected to climb down that,' Molly whispered. She swallowed. Victoria knew the two things her friend hated most were climbing and heights.

Her section waited patiently for the ship's officer to speak; he stood by the rail to address them and his voice was strong and clear when he started. They were told they had to report to that position, wearing their hats, overcoats and lifebelts, and await instructions. At this point his voice rose almost to a screech.

'Did you hear that? On no account are you to attempt to descend the rope. You must wait for instructions. And whatever you do, don't jump. For God's sake don't ever – ever – jump.' The man's eyes rolled wildly and he appeared to shake.

What was wrong with him? A man standing pressed close behind her whispered in her ear. 'That poor blighter has been torpedoed several times and the last time people jumped and the boats went down on top of them.'

She glanced over the side at the dark, uninviting sea and shivered. Why would anyone, however frightened, have chosen to jump rather than wait for instructions? There was the crackle of the loudspeaker as it burst into speech again.

'Smoking on deck after sundown is forbidden. Blackout and portholes must not be tampered with on any account.'

As Victoria and her group began to move away,

the loudspeaker continued to tell them about the disposal of waste items.

'Good God! What a horrible thought. To think that anything, even a used sanitary towel, could be a clue to a waiting U-boat. I'm not looking forward to this journey. The more I hear the less I like the sound of it.'

'Molly, you're overreacting. There are far fewer U-boats around than there were, and we're being escorted by a flotilla of battleships. I'm certain we'll arrive safely.' She smiled encouragingly at her friend. 'I'm far more bothered by the instruction we have to wear slacks over our pyjamas every night. It doesn't seem a very practical way to carry on, but I suppose if there was an emergency we wouldn't want to be running around on deck in our nightclothes.'

It was so cold on deck the girls decided to return to their cabin; despite its claustrophobic atmosphere this was preferable to freezing outside.

'Did you notice we're positioned inside the circle of boats, and nearest to the aircraft carrier? Does that mean we're in the safest place, do you think?' Mary asked.

Angela answered immediately. 'Of course it does. We're a passenger ship, unarmed; we have to be protected. Now, let's forget about U-boats and Germans and make the most of a few weeks without work.'

* * *

Life on board the ship soon settled into a routine. Fresh water came on for thirty-minute intervals twice a day, at six in the morning and evening. When the bell rang first thing Victoria fell out of her berth, washed and went back to dry whilst sitting on her bunk. For three hours every day, from nine o'clock until noon, everyone was obliged to be on deck.

'I thought we were supposed to be up here doing lifeboat drill?' Angela, as always, was quick to spot a flaw in the planning.

A passing sailor was happy to stop and answer. 'It's the only way the captain can make sure the ship gets a breather, miss. But you don't have to stand; you can sit on your hats if you want.'

Victoria was grateful that as long as she remained in her place in the line she was free to read, smoke or play cards. Barbara produced a Ludo board and they played endless games as they sat, lifejackets and greatcoats on, outside in the freezing February fog.

The rest of the day was spent standing in line. She queued for tea, queued for drinks and also to buy anything in the ship's shop. She also had to wait her turn to use the bathroom and to wash her clothes with seawater soap.

The evenings were spent in companionable chat. As she lay on her bunk playing word games, telling stories and talking, she came to think of these times as the most enjoyable of the long, tedious voyage. The days passed and after a while she lost track of the date and didn't know how long they'd been sailing.

They appeared to be travelling in a straight line, but one day the sun was on the west and the next in the east. The temperature was becoming noticeably warmer; sitting on deck during the day was possible without her greatcoat on.

'How many men do you think there are for every woman on board the ship?' Jenny asked one morning.

Victoria followed her glance and everywhere she looked there seemed to be the grey-blue of RAF uniforms, and the khaki of soldiers – theirs was the only female contingent in sight.

'I think there are WAAFs and ATS somewhere on the ship, but I've never seen them,' Molly said.

'How many have you talked to, Barbara?' Victoria

asked, with a smile. Barbara was the flirtatious member of the group.

Barbara grinned. 'About a dozen, but I didn't just talk to them; otherwise we wouldn't have extra biscuits and cigarettes now, would we?'

She wasn't sure what Barbara was doing was strictly moral, but in the circumstances she supposed it was a fair exchange. A quick fumble and a kiss, and in return the gift of a pack of cigarettes or biscuits. At least no money was involved.

One afternoon she was leaning on the rails, the sun shining pleasantly on her back, Molly at her side, when she saw the unmistakable shape of Gibraltar. The convoy swung south keeping the skyline of North Africa on the starboard side and sailed east.

'Well, at least we know where we are now, Molly.'

'Yes, but how much further do you think it is to where we're going?'

'I've no idea. My geography is useless. You'd better ask Angela – she appears to know everything.' She glanced at her watch. 'Good grief, we're on duty in the sickbay in thirty minutes. We'd better go down and tidy ourselves up.'

* * *

Victoria was busy dressing the wound of a sailor who had cut his leg the day before.

'Thanks, ma'am, that's a lot more comfortable than when the doc did it. When do you think you can take the stitches out?'

'It's healing well, so with any luck I expect I can remove them by the end of the week. Why, are you in a hurry to get back on duty?'

'Not likely – it's a cushy billet coming down here.'

Just as the young man completed his sentence the sound of a klaxon indicating that they were under attack was heard throughout the ship. For moment she froze, her mind going blank, forgetting all the drills she'd done over the past two weeks. Molly jerked her back to life.

'Bloody hell! That's all we need. Come on, we've got to get these blokes up on deck. They'll not stand a chance if we sink, stuck down here.'

Galvanised into action, Victoria turned to the sailor. He was already on his feet and waiting for his orders. 'Quickly, help me get Bill onto the stretcher. He can't walk with a broken leg.'

Bill was only too eager to scramble onto the canvas. 'Here, take the front end of this; I'll carry the other. Molly, can you help Sergeant Smithson?'

'We'll manage. It's a good thing there's only three of them down here at the moment.'

Somehow the party negotiated the narrow passageway and staggered up the stairs. Outside it was dark, the air full of choking black smoke, and the klaxon continued to scream abuse at them. The boat appeared to be yawing from side to side and people were running in all directions.

A strong hand in the small of her back gave her a violent shove forward. The young sailor who was holding the other end of the stretcher didn't have a chance. The canvas caught him in the small of his back and he went flat. The patient landed on top of him and Victoria landed on the patient. Then everything went even darker.

For a moment she lay there, her heart pounding so hard everyone must have been able to hear it. 'I'm terribly sorry, but I can't move at the moment.'

A rich chuckle filled the stygian black. 'Don't worry about it, ma'am, this is the best treat I've had all year.'

She blushed; she was aware even through the thickness of her khaki uniform that she was lying in a most indelicate place.

'Are you all right, Molly? You're very quiet over there.'

Molly's voice echoed from a few feet away. 'Bloody hell! Bugger me! Sergeant Smithson and I only just made it. Do you think that the enormous thump was a torpedo?'

She was about to answer when suddenly it was daylight again. Three grinning faces peered down.

'Come along, ladies and gentlemen. It was only a drill, and the captain says we did all right.'

Good grief! They had been under a lifeboat. Whoever it was who had pushed her forward had also dropped the boat over them once they were safely on the deck. Hastily she rolled to one side and stood up, not daring to meet the eyes of the injured soldier lying on the stretcher at her feet.

Molly jumped up, but left her patient – who was suffering from a chest infection – to recover his breath before offering him her arm. 'Well, that was exciting, I don't think. You'd think they'd have better things to do than play silly buggers.'

Her remark was overheard by an officer checking everything was as it should be. 'It's far better you have some experience of what it might actually be like if we were hit, than leave it to the real thing, don't you think?' His steely eyes bored into them, making Victoria feel small and traitorous for complaining. Molly hung her head and mumbled an apology. Victoria watched the officer stride off, no doubt to see who else he could humiliate.

'Come along, we'd better get you all back downstairs. I expect your dressing will need redoing; I hardly had time to fasten it before we were sent up here...' She snapped her mouth shut, before she could complete the sentence.

Molly offered her arm to the coughing sergeant and he gratefully accepted. The sailor grabbed the front of the stretcher and Victoria took her place at the rear once more. The trek back downstairs seemed longer and more tortuous than their exit.

When they returned she carefully assisted Billy to his bed, checked his leg had come to no harm and then told the sailor to sit down by the treatment table. She heard Molly settling her patient back into his bunk.

'I should take off your greatcoat and lifejacket, ma'am, and sit down and have a cup of tea.'

She stared at the cheery orderly who had just come in carrying a tray with steaming mugs. She hadn't realised she was still wearing full kit until he mentioned it.

'How stupid of me. I'm afraid I'm not very good in an emergency.'

* * *

That evening the incident was regaled to the rest of the group with much laughing and disparaging remarks about jumped-up officers. Whatever the reasoning behind the drill, and it must be sound, it had just made her more scared of the real thing rather than less.

The weather was getting hotter as they ploughed on their way through the Mediterranean. She was bitterly disappointed by the Suez Canal, having expected something far grander. The waterway was little more than an overgrown ditch. She was impressed by the row of black-garbed Bedouins who had watched impassively from the backs of camels as they slipped through.

That afternoon a German spotter plane found them and the atmosphere on the ship changed dramatically. Nobody admitted to having seen the little black shape following them high in the sky, but they all knew he was there. She didn't have to ask what it meant. There could be German U-boats, or fighter planes, coming at any moment to try and sink them. When three days later, in sight of their destination, the plane departed she breathed a sigh of relief.

Soon after this the convoy split. The aircraft carrier, the other passenger ship, two corvettes and two of the battleships veered away heading for India, so Angela told her. Her heart followed them. How she wished she was on one of those distant ships, but Africa was her destination and the coastline was rapidly approaching.

Her spirits lifted at the thought of being able to feel dry land under her feet once more. Africa wasn't home, but it was a lot closer to India than England. Her eyes filled – and a lot further from Amelia.

14

ACROSS COUNTRY

Victoria stood beside her friend, holdall between her knees, greatcoat folded over her arm and tin hat and gas mask dangling round her neck. She was pleased to see Dora was one of the two sisters in charge of their party.

'Well, ladies, here we are. I'm sorry to tell you your draft is dividing up into groups of four. It's unfortunate we have to split you, but we've tried to keep you with at least one of your messmates. It's a long time since any fresh nursing staff arrived in Africa and we're needed in several different places.'

Molly shuffled closer to Victoria. 'Well, at least we'll stay together, even if we lose the other four.'

'I shall miss them, but as long as we've got each other, we can cope with anything, can't we?'

The *Stratheden* received an unexpectedly lavish welcome. When a principal matron boarded and embraced both sisters with tears streaming down her cheeks Victoria understood exactly why she had been sent to nurse in this distant country.

The draft disembarked and she was directed with Molly and Dora and half the draft into the arms of a welcoming committee. They didn't have time to more than wave to the four girls they had shared the last three months with as they vanished with the second sister.

The two ladies designated to take care of them ushered them into a sturdy tin hut and plied them with large mugs of tea. Sugar was offered in bowls; it was a long time since she had seen such largesse. A basket of oranges and bananas was offered and they were encouraged to help themselves. When a fruit cake made with fresh eggs and real fruit appeared Victoria felt her eyes fill.

'Thank you so much – you cannot imagine how it feels to have left a war-torn Britain, where everything is rationed, and arrive here in sunlight and warmth and to be offered things we haven't seen for years.'

'My dears, we fully understand. That's why we

have made such an effort. Please, if you don't wish to eat the cake now, take a generous slice each and save it for later.' The smiling middle-aged woman was dressed in a dull, floral dress that reminded Victoria painfully of her journey, five years before, when she had left India as a radiant, pregnant bride.

Molly whispered as they left, 'It doesn't seem right, us having so much when back at home they're living on practically nothing.'

Dora overheard and was quick to answer. 'Believe me, Nurse Smith, a few slices of cake and a bit of fruit will hardly compensate for the hardships and horrors you're going to experience before you get back to Blighty.'

She wanted to reassure her friend things might be different, poverty more acute perhaps, but people all over the world were the same. Everyone had the same needs and Molly would soon get used to living without running water and a flushing lavatory. But she couldn't. No one knew she'd spent the first seventeen years of her life in India, and even to reassure Molly she wasn't going to reveal any of her secrets.

They were driven straight to the station and told to wait in the shade of a dilapidated building for their trunks to arrive. The twenty or so girls collapsed like rag dolls, their strength already sapped by the humidity and heat.

She was glad Dora was travelling with them as this meant she could remain passive and the older woman could tell them what to do.

'It appears there's a train arriving in a couple of hours and we're to catch it. We're being sent across Kenya to Nairobi and will then be attached to various military hospitals.'

'Blimey! That sounds a long way away. I didn't know we had any military in Nairobi,' Molly said as she attempted to mop the sweat from her face with a khaki handkerchief.

'We have bases everywhere. Have you never heard the saying that "the sun never sets on the British Empire"?'

'No, Sister, I haven't. I'm not even sure what it means, but it's too blooming hot to worry about it. I'm in the army and do as I'm told like everyone else.'

'Not like every other member; never forget that you're an officer, and must appear calm and in control at all times however frightened and confused you might be.' Dora marched off to oversee the arrival of the boxes, leaving them to mull over what she'd said.

'I'm not officer material, Victoria, whatever she says. I'm just an ordinary nurse and can't be anything else. God! It's bloody hot – even worse than the Red Sea.'

* * *

Victoria was revelling in the warmth, feeling her frozen bones thawing after five years of living in dull, cold Britain. 'We'll get used to it. In fact if you think about it, which do you prefer, heat or cold?'

Molly yawned hugely and closed her eyes. 'I would prefer to get out of these clothes and into my tropical kit. What are we supposed to do with our greatcoats, tin hat and gas mask over here?'

'I've no idea and I don't care. The one good thing about being in the army is there's always someone around to tell you what to do.'

She stared out of the window enjoying the lush landscape of Africa. However, after twenty-four hours the novelty had long since gone and she dozed and chatted in turn with Molly and her four new companions. Eventually the train steamed into Nairobi.

'Good God!' The girl nearest the window – Victoria had already forgotten her name – exclaimed. 'There's bunting up, and a group of dignitaries waiting to meet us.'

Pandemonium reigned as they all tried to comb

their hair and straighten their wilting uniforms. She was conscious she was the only one unfazed by the heat. It was only a matter of time before Molly commented.

Again the draft was divided but Victoria wasn't parted from her friend. The group of ten nurses were taken to the mess where she discovered why they had been made such a fuss of. Apparently a large number of nurses had drowned in the Indian Ocean when their ship was torpedoed. Their draft was a replacement for the women who had died. She realised her arrival was viewed as a sign by this group that they were not being ignored.

The next day she attended a service of thanksgiving at Nairobi Cathedral. Apart from the stifling heat she could have been attending an English church. The priest in his sermon talked of Florence Nightingale and thanked God for the safe arrival of the nurses after so long.

'Makes you feel like royalty, doesn't it?'

Victoria heard Molly's comment and was forced to hide a smile. If only her friend knew how much truth there was in that casual remark. 'I hope they don't make a big fuss of us. I'm here to work, not be treated like a VIP.'

'I doubt anyone will realise we are nurses. They

are used to seeing the QAs dressed in scarlet and grey, not combat clothes like these.'

'I hope you're right, Molly. The sooner I'm attached to a ward and doing the job I joined up for, the happier I'll be.'

* * *

The hospital she was sent to was set in the outskirts of the city and from the grounds of the sisters' mess. Victoria could gaze out and see Kilimanjaro in the distance, its peak snow-capped even in May. She longed for the mountains of India and prayed somehow she might be transferred there before the end of the war. Their living quarters were primitive compared to the large, airy bungalow used for recreation.

'Good grief! Is this where we've got to sleep? They look like kennels.' Molly was not pleased.

Victoria had wandered over to look at the tiny room, which contained washbasins and showers. 'Then don't come over here and look at the ablutions because they're even worse than the rooms.'

'I'm bursting to spend a penny – that wooden building behind the showers looks like a sanitary block. Shall we go and try them out?'

She followed, waiting to hear what Molly would make of using a lavatory that was basically a deep pit in which a constant low fire burnt.

'A bit strange – but remarkably non-smelly. Victoria, are you out there?'

'No, I'm in the cubicle next to you. Did you get a blast of hot air as soon as you sat down?'

'I did – and I suppose I'll have to get used to it, like everything else in this place.'

When she emerged from the washroom Victoria discovered an African boy waiting outside one of the cubicles. This was obviously the batman she'd been promised. Smiling she pointed to her boxes and the youngster nodded vigorously and carried them into one of the stable-like rooms. She could hear similar sounds of unpacking in the accommodation on the left of hers and knew Molly was also settling in.

She had been told to report to Ward B as soon as she was organised. She glanced at her watch – a little after two o'clock. She stood back to admire her living quarters. With the camp bed made up neatly, her spare uniform hanging from a peg and her personal bits and pieces laid out on the small wooden box that served as dressing table and desk, the cubicle didn't look quite so inhospitable. When the hurricane lamp was on it would almost be cosy. The mosquito net hung limply from the ceiling warning her of what to expect after dark.

'Are you ready, Molly? We'd better get over to Ward B and report to Sister Digby.'

A flaming-red head appeared in the doorway. 'Righto! We need to take anything with us?'

'Like what?'

'Tin hat and gas mask.'

'Have a heart, Molly. Do you think we're likely to be gassed or bombed in the middle of an African jungle?'

'Point taken. Still, you never know in the army. Do you actually know where to go?'

Victoria grinned; her young helper, Sami, had explained by gesture and pantomime the where-abouts of the ward they sought. 'Follow me, Nurse Smith. I have had clear directions.'

She was pleasantly surprised to find Ward B was precisely where she expected it to be. The building was little more than a Nissen hut with curved corrugated roof and French doors at either end. Windows were positioned haphazardly down either side.

'Blimey! It seems strange the sisters' mess is in better nick than the ward.'

Victoria smiled. 'I suppose the thinking behind it

is the nursing staff are here a lot longer than the patients.'

Someone had alerted Sister Digby and she appeared at the open doors to greet them. 'Welcome, Staff Nurse Jones, Staff Nurse Smith. You cannot believe how pleased I am to see you.'

There were tears in her eyes and for a horrible moment Victoria thought she was going to be embraced yet again. 'We're glad to be here, ma'am, and eager to start work.' She glanced down the ward and to her astonishment saw all but three of the twenty-four beds were unoccupied.

'Don't worry, my dear, you'll find things are run differently here. All but the bedridden prefer to spend their days outside somewhere. It's almost three o'clock, time for drug round, so the orderly will bring them back.'

She exchanged glances with Molly who looked equally bemused. A native orderly appeared, his teeth a flash of white in a black face. He shot past and stood on the concrete path, then clapping his hands round his mouth he bellowed. 'Wardie B. Wardie B.'

Sister Digby called them over. 'They'll be back in a minute. Come along, I want to show you where the drugs are kept, the sluice room and storerooms. There are two orderlies and two general factotums, which means one of each per shift. The MO, Doctor Beaumont, does his rounds at ten o'clock every morning. There are two doctors and a surgeon at this hospital; not nearly enough of course, but we have to make do.'

She followed her mentor from room to room nodding and speaking when required, but scarcely able to assimilate the strangeness of everything. Whilst they were in the stock cupboard there was the sound of voices outside the door. Molly nudged her and raised her eyebrows comically.

'The wanderers return.' Sister Digby smiled unaware of their suppressed giggles. 'Come along, nurses, let me introduce you to your patients. You have two malaria cases, several infected wounds, one pneumonia – he's the chap who stayed in bed – two jungle fever and a jaundice.'

When they came out of the stock cupboard every bed was occupied by a smiling black face. Victoria hadn't realised how many Africans were a part of the British military operation. She and Molly followed Sister Digby around the ward, being introduced to each patient in turn. She was asked to administer the drugs and so checked each patient's name on the list against the name at head of the bed before handing out the medicine.

'Mind you, you have to be careful. When I got here two years ago I gave the drugs to someone I thought was the patient, but it turned out to be his brother. The wretched man had been visiting and was just keeping the bed occupied in case anybody else took it during his brother's absence.'

Victoria thought this tale highly unlikely, but it made a good anecdote. They returned to the nurses' station, a table at the end of the long room, and she and Molly sat down on two chairs hastily fetched by the orderly.

'Well, I don't suppose this is what you expected, or what you're used to, but it's how things are out here. You two are going to be running Ward B whilst I take some leave. I've not had a day off in over six months and once you're settled I'm going to have two weeks' leave.'

Her throat closed and the weight of unwanted responsibility settled over her shoulders. How could they possibly run this alien place on their own with only a couple of shifts to acclimatise?

Sister Digby looked from one to the other. 'Don't look so shocked, girls – you'll cope wonderfully well. You will have seen far worse during the Blitz than you'll get here. Now, who is going to take the first three weeks of nights and who the day shifts?'

'I'll do nights, if you like, Molly. I don't sleep very well anyway.'

Molly nodded her thanks. 'Do we get no time off at all?'

'You'll do the three weeks and then, when I return, you'll get three days' leave together.'

'Victoria, we'll never see each other. We'll be like ships that pass in the night.'

'Or in the early morning,' Victoria added, her smile rueful.

'You'll change shift pattern after your leave. Now, as you're going to be doing nights, Staff Nurse Jones, I suggest you go back to your quarters and try and get some sleep. I want you to report back at seven thirty.'

* * *

Sister Digby was right; it was much easier nursing in Ward B than it had it had been at St Thomas'. However, she missed the camaraderie of the other nurses and especially Molly. The only time they met was when they handed over at the beginning and end of their shifts.

The three weeks passed and she was looking forward to spending an uninterrupted forty-eight hours with Molly and having the time to catch up on her news. She had adjusted to the primitive living quarters. Her cramped room was bearable only if she spent the minimum time there; she went to the sisters' mess to eat whenever she had the time or energy to do so. She was pleased to see other members of her draft, but it wasn't the same as seeing Molly.

Sister Digby returned from her two weeks' furlough a new woman, but was working as a relief in Ward O whilst the two girls were running Ward B for her.

Victoria finished her stint first. She handed over to Molly as she had done every morning for the past three weeks.

'I'm going to get some sleep if I can, then I shall have a shower and meet you in the mess. I've arranged for a lift to Nairobi tomorrow morning. Is that okay?'

Molly nodded. 'Yes, sounds smashing. We ought to see some of the sights whilst we're here I suppose.'

She managed to sleep for four hours, about average for her. She got up and decided to use the showers. It was a good time to go in as the day shift was working and most of night shift was still asleep. Having grown up in India she knew the danger of lurking spiders and snakes. She had persuaded Molly to sleep with her shoes tucked under the mattress every night just to make sure nothing unpleasant crawled in unannounced. Her friend hadn't questioned her superior knowledge, which meant for once she didn't have to lie.

She sat up, checking the floor, before reaching under her mattress and sliding her feet into her shoes. She slipped her arms into her cotton dressing gown and gathering up her washbag, she left for the showers.

As she stepped in she saw a suspicious shiver of movement in the far corner, the darkest dampest corner. She recognised a snake when she saw one. She edged out and went back to her room to light her hurricane lamp. Holding the light aloft she examined the far corner of the shower. Sure enough there was a long black snake. Was it the dreaded black mamba?

She'd watched house servants, and even her ayah, deal with snakes when they'd entered the house, but she'd never had to do so herself. She knew these serpents moved quickly and that their bite was usually fatal. No time to fetch help – she'd be dead before it arrived. She hesitated in the doorway to the shower. There was the sound of bare feet approaching and she turned to find Sami, her clean uniform, freshly starched, hanging over his arm.

She pointed to the snake. 'Is that a mamba, Sami?'

The boy pursed his lips and then began shaking his head vigorously. 'No, no, not a bad snake at all, missy.' Before she could stop him he handed her the uniform and stepped past her. In his bare feet, and without even a stick for protection, he reached down and, grabbing the snake by the tail, he threw it over the corrugated iron side of the ablutions building.

It still looked like a krait to her. 'Are you sure that wasn't a dangerous snake, Sami?'

He beamed. 'Snake all gone now, missy; have nice shower.'

He'd risked his life in order to keep her safe. She was immeasurably moved by his gesture and patted his shoulder as he went past. 'Thank you, Sami. I'll not forget what you've done.'

* * *

When she told Molly about the snake she was horrified. 'Well, I'm going to shower in the sisters' mess. I know we're not supposed to, it's visitors only, but I'm not going in our block ever again.'

'You're going to have to, Molly. Where else can

you go? You can't not shower; it's just too hot and sticky.'

'Then I'll use the shower block at the far end of the compound, the one near the perimeter fence. I noticed it today. It looks clean and I don't think anyone uses it very often.'

She wasn't sure this was a good idea, but in the pleasure and excitement of spending the next three days with her dearest friend, she forgot about her reservations.

15

ON THE MOVE

Victoria and Molly arrived at the sisters' mess to find a group nurses gathered at the noticeboard.

'Something's up. Shall we go and have a dekko?'

'Yes, we'd better. Must be something important to cause such a fuss.'

It was notice of a draft and after scanning the list of sixty or so names Victoria saw they were both on it. She turned to her friend in some surprise.

'Look at that! We're scheduled to go overseas.' She could barely suppress the excitement that swept over her. Overseas could mean only one thing – moving closer to India – if not home itself.

'We've only just got here, Victoria. Why are we being sent somewhere else?'

One of the women in front put her finger to her lips, shaking her head. 'Come over here, and I'll tell you,' she whispered dramatically. 'We're not supposed to speak about these things where anyone can hear.'

Victoria was puzzled. How could the enemy possibly know what was said in the sisters' mess in the middle of Africa?

Their informant turned, her face serious. 'Didn't you hear about the nurses who were drowned in the Indian Ocean a while back?' Victoria and Molly nodded. 'We are the draft who is going to replace them.' She paused, checking both of them were paying attention. 'Everyone says talking about the trip to India caused them to be torpedoed.'

'We're going to India? That's even further from England, isn't it, Victoria?'

'It is, but from what I've heard there's less jungle in India and loads of people speak English. That should make our lives easier.'

'You'd better go and see when you have to report for a fitting of your new uniforms,' Freda, their helpful informant, told them. Victoria, who was taller than Molly, was able to read over the heads of the other girls. She saw that they had to report the next day to a tailor's in Nairobi and also to the officers' shop.

'No wonder I had no difficulty arranging a lift into Nairobi tomorrow. I bet the driver already knew lots of us would have to go in to order uniform.' She noticed the group around the noticeboard was drifting away. 'We better go and collect the necessary chits, for we'll get nothing tomorrow without them.'

Molly vanished to have her illegal shower and Victoria bagged a table in the canteen. At least when she eventually returned to India she would be able to get real vegetarian food. Henry had told her, all those years ago, she would have to learn to eat whatever she was given in case anyone suspected her mixed ancestry. He implied only foreigners didn't eat meat with every meal.

Whilst living at The Rookery it had been easier; initially she claimed morning sickness gave her an aversion to flesh and then told Marion that she actually preferred meat-free meals. As meat was one of the first things to be rationed, that suited everyone.

However it had been more difficult once she'd moved into the nurses' home attached to St Thomas's Hospital. She could hardly turn down the food she was offered and she needed to eat in order to stay fit enough to work twelve-hour shifts. Over the years she gradually forced her rebellious digestion and moral scruples into the depths of her subconscious. This allowed her to eat rabbit and chicken, but so far she'd managed to avoid cow or pig. No Indian ever ate either of those.

When they arrived at the officers' shop Victoria presented her chit for fresh underwear. Mindful of the instructions not to reveal their destination Victoria told the sergeant they were being sent up-country.

He held up a pair of knickers and waved them in the air. 'These are not for upcountry, ma'am, they're Far East issue. They're cellular weave, see?'

Clutching her parcel of cellular weave underwear she left the shop, not sure whether to laugh or feel embarrassed at having had her knickers waved in the air for all to see. Molly was still sniggering.

The second slip sent them to an Indian tailor to collect khaki drill slacks and bush jackets. These were made to measure, a novelty for Molly, and a welcome reminder of things past for her. She slipped her arm through Molly's and together they strolled down the broad street admiring the many smart shops, uniformly owned by white people.

'It seems strange to see the windows without all that blooming tape.'

Victoria agreed. 'Yes, apart from the number of uniforms around, you could forget there was a war on.'

The two largest buildings in the city were the Stanley Hotel and the Bank of India – these didn't impress either of them.

'When do we have to return to collect our kit?' Molly asked as she spooned her last mouthful of ice cream at Jack Frost's Parlour.

'He said by the end of the week, don't you remember? He apologised for taking so long.'

'Well, that's no good is it? We'll be back on duty by then and not get any more leave until we've done three weeks.'

'I'm sure that's been thought of. If we're about to be sent overseas, perhaps, like the time before we left England, we'll not be on formal duty and have plenty of spare time.'

* * *

This proved to be the case. The hanging about, whilst being obliged to stay within the hospital confines unless given permission to collect uniform or kit, became tedious after a time. As Victoria had predicted they were taken off the roster and merely worked as relief in different wards when other nurses needed free time.

One night, after a particularly riotous party put on by the British sergeants to cheer them up, they returned in the small hours to find a note pinned to their pillows saying they were to be called at four o'clock and to be packed and ready to leave.

There were cries and exclamations of horror as nurse after nurse found the same orders. Molly shouted over the cubicle wall to her.

'Blimey! We'll never be ready in time. Are we supposed to take everything with us, including our greatcoats and gas masks?'

'We'd better. I expect some idiot will expect to see them in a few months and if we don't have them we'll be put on a charge.'

She didn't bother to go to bed but lay down fully dressed under the mosquito net and waited to be called. The matron herself came to collect the sixty or so nurses who were leaving and took them to the mess for the last time. They were served a breakfast of hard-boiled eggs and tea.

She scrambled into one of the waiting ambulances after Molly and heard the door being locked behind her. Thirty bumpy minutes later they arrived at their destination. Victoria was first off and in the early morning mist could just make out two sweeping railway tracks. Not a station, just a place to load and unload troops. She stood next to Molly shivering, glad she had worn her greatcoat. Victoria wasn't sure if it was excitement or anticipation causing her tremors.

'Shall we go and get a cup of tea? They seem to be serving some over by that old oil drum with a fire in it.'

Victoria wasn't too worried about the refreshments. She'd seen the bottom of the bucket when they'd been offered tea on her previous train journey and she'd have to be desperate before she drank such a brew again.

Being a seasoned traveller she now had her irons (tin cup and plate, plus cutlery) stored safely in her haversack. She felt it might appear unsociable to remain the only one not accepting the free tea offered by the British soldiers, so she joined the queue. When she finally got a drink it was surprisingly palatable.

Eventually the train arrived and they piled in, this time only four to a compartment. Molly and she shared with two girls they had become friendly with during the month they had stayed at the hospital in Nairobi.

The train arrived at Mombasa and after collecting their belongings they settled down for another long wait. She was aware there were hundreds of African troops pouring off the train. They were warned by a passing disembodied voice that there was to be no loud talking or any singing or smoking.

'I'm beginning to get used to hanging around in uncomfortable and boring places,' she told Molly. 'At least we're still together, but I wonder how long that will last?'

'I've spoken to Him upstairs, and he's given me His assurance that for us "*it's till death us do part*" just like true love.' The girls giggled, knowing that they had no energy for romance.

Dawn came before they began the embarkation. This time the cabin they were allocated was twice the size of the one they'd shared on the way over and only had four berths. The ship sailed and life settled down into its customary routine. One of the sisters volunteered to help with the African troops, who were prostrate on the deck with seasickness. She was smartly rebuffed by one of the officers, who told her African orderlies could cope better with these things themselves.

The only relief to the boredom was when the MO on board decided to inoculate all the troops against plague. She and Molly stood swabbing and jabbing in turns until the whole ship had been done.

The ship finally arrived in Colombo on the island of Ceylon and anchored in the middle of the bay. Victoria leant on the rail, drinking in the landscape. The azure sea, the white buildings and green palm trees silhouetted around a golden arc of sand, were achingly familiar. The view was stunning – her long return was nearing its end.

The draft was split again, most of them going to a hospital in Colombo; the rest, including Victoria and Molly, were taken by ambulance to a large hospital on the outskirts of the city. This building was a great improvement on the place they'd been to in Nairobi.

'This looks more like it. Do you know it reminds me of the sort of place Florence Nightingale built?' Molly said as she stood beside her, waiting to be directed to their accommodation.

'Yes, it's got several detached wards and they all seem to be linked by a central corridor. Look, isn't that a covered walkway running round the back? Thank God! That means we won't get wet when it's the monsoon.'

A smart British corporal arrived to take them to their quarters. Victoria noticed the hospital was in a dip, but the recreation hall and residential buildings were a short distance away on top of a grassy bank, the two linked together by a stone staircase. In the distance she spotted a few ramshackle buildings hugging the perimeter fence.

'Look at this: little thatched houses. They certainly look a lot better than the last things we had to sleep in,' Molly said.

The orderly grinned. 'These are called bandas, ma'am, nice and snug and keep the rain out. You've got a lovely little veranda to sit on outside your cubicle as well.'

Victoria smiled. How many of them would actually get any time to sit on the "lovely little verandas"? Inside the space was not much bigger than before but it was drier and didn't smell so damp.

'Don't we get a boy to help us?' Victoria asked their guide.

'Sorry, ma'am. You get a cleaner and your laundry done, but that's it, I'm afraid.'

'Thank you, corporal. I'm sure we can manage to unpack for ourselves.' Her parents would be amazed to see how domesticated she'd become since leaving India. Five years ago she'd not known how to make a bed.

Molly hated the huts. She swore she could hear snakes and other things slithering about on the roof all night and even the cheerful chipmunks upset her. Victoria tried to reassure her, but mess gossip about the pythons, the krait and the other poisonous snakes that abounded didn't help her friend's fears.

This time she was split from Molly. They were given duties in different wards. After their first shift she got back to the banda to hear Molly sobbing in her cubicle.

'What's wrong? Whatever's happened?'

'I can't stand it. This place is even worse than Africa. Those ceiling drapes – do you know why they're heaving and moving all the time?'

She understood immediately. 'It's the snakes catching the rats. But they don't fall through – they can't, and it's nature's way of keeping the hospital free of vermin. You'll have to get used to it. We're here to do a job; just concentrate on that and pray that the war will soon be over and we can go home.'

'I'd rather be on the blooming front, being bombed and fired at than out here with creepy-crawlies and snakes.'

'You wouldn't say that if you were actually there. Now, if you're feeling better let's go over to the mess and get drunk.'

* * *

After a few weeks she began to believe Molly had accepted her posting and was becoming more relaxed about things. However, when one of the girls emerged semi-naked from the ablutions block screaming that there was a huge python in one of the shower cubicles, Molly was back to square one.

'I'm going to find somewhere else to shower, somewhere away from the trees, in a clearing, where I can be sure there are no snakes hiding.'

'Don't you remember what Sister Digby said, and Matron, about using someone else's shower block?'

'Back in Africa, in Nairobi, I used the showers over by the perimeter fence and nobody said a word about that.'

'Yes, but perhaps you noticed your boy always went with you and even when you couldn't see him, he was waiting close by. He kept you safe, like Sami looked after me.'

'I don't care, I'm not using these showers unless I'm certain there are no snakes in there.'

'How about if I check the showers before you go in? I'm not bothered by them.'

'All right – I promise I'll not wander off. But you must promise to always check before I go in? Is that a deal?'

* * *

The following week she changed to nights but Molly remained on the day shift. This meant they would hardly see each other, unless their rest days coincided. Her friend said no more about using different showers. Hopefully she had persuaded Molly it was more dangerous to wander off alone than risk sharing one's shower with a snake.

She'd been going into the showers first to check they were safe, but now they were on different shifts Molly might go back on her word. For a few days she managed to persuade one of the other nurses to take over the responsibility and believed the crisis was over. However, when the nurse was also transferred to nights Molly was left isolated. She was, for some unknown reason the only nurse in the banda still doing a day shift.

One Wednesday, no different from any others, Victoria was waiting outside her ward as usual to give Molly a hug as she trudged off duty. However, that evening she missed her friend and was forced to go in to begin her shift without their customary embrace and exchange of news.

She was just settling her last patient, with the help of her two orderlies, when the night was disturbed by shouting and then men pounded past the ward. The hideous rattle of gunfire exploded the silence. Forcing herself to remain calm, she completed her routine at the bedside and with an anxious smile at her orderlies, hurried back down the ward to see what all the fuss was about.

It was black as pitch and away from the glow of the overhead lights she could see nothing. On the far side, by the perimeter fence, she thought she could hear voices and see torches moving about. She heard soft steps as her corporal arrived at her side.

'I reckon some bugger's tried to climb over the fence to steal drugs, ma'am. From the gunfire I reckon they shot him. Serves the bastard right.'

She didn't answer immediately. 'But why would they look for drugs over there? It's the residential side of the compound, not the medical.'

The corporal scratched his head. 'Not a clue, ma'am. But I expect we'll know what happened before the end of the shift.'

No doubt he was right. She must contain her curiosity and return to her duties. She was so busy that the rest of her shift flashed by and she forgot about the drama of the night before. She waited, as was customary, by the table, to hand over. Instead of the solitary nurse she was expecting Matron strode in as well.

'Nurse Jones, would you like to come into the office? I'm afraid I have some difficult news to give you.' She followed the matron into the office, a feeling of dread pinning her to the floor.

Matron looked kindly at her. 'I think you'd better sit down, my dear.'

She did as she was told. Her face was numb, as though her blood had drained to her feet.

'My dear, I'm sure you heard the gunfire last night. An intruder climbed into the compound.' The woman stopped, obviously having difficulty with the next few words. 'I'm afraid there was a terrible incident. Nurse Smith was murdered by the intruder. We have no idea what she was doing over that side. It is a terrible tragedy, a dreadful waste of a young life.'

Victoria stared at her. The words Molly had said so casually such a short time ago reverberated through her head – 'till death us do part' – 'till death us do part' – 'till death us do part'. She closed her eyes and was carried towards the blackness she had lived in after Henry's death. She raised her head, swallowing her tears.

'She didn't like snakes.' That was all she could manage before grief overwhelmed her.

16

MOVING ON

The aftermath of the horrible event changed everything. Molly, by her death, had become an army nurse, no longer the laughing, red-headed Londoner she had come to know and love for the past six months. She had metamorphosed into a soldier who deserved a military funeral and everything that entailed.

Victoria got no special treatment, apart from Matron having given her the news personally. After that she was expected to get on with her job like everybody else. Her dearest friend was a statistic, another casualty of this awful war.

The funeral was held the following day – in the heat of Colombo it wouldn't do to leave a corpse lying around too long. She was given time to attend, but refused. She didn't want to see her friend's mortal remains interred on foreign soil so far from her beloved England. She didn't even have Molly's home address, so couldn't write to Mr and Mrs Smith and tell them how close she'd been to their daughter.

Her eyes filled and she blinked them away. She had a ward to run, there was a war on, and she was here to do her bit. Lots of people died. Henry had died, but she was still alive and had to get on with it.

Although she remained efficient she no longer went to the recreation hall or joined in any of the parties or excursions. She was obliged to go and eat in the canteen, but always sat alone and answered monosyllabically when spoken to.

About a month after Molly's death the first of the monsoon rain fell whilst a group of the nurses had been visiting Colombo. They were full of the experience when they returned and she couldn't help but overhear them.

'It was amazing wasn't it? To be walking along in pouring rain that doesn't reach the pavement,' one of them exclaimed.

'I think it must be like flying above the clouds. You know, when the plane is in sunshine and down below it's raining, but this time it was the other way up.'

She couldn't resist being drawn into the conversation. 'Did you have to walk through mist up to your knees?'

Ann, the older of the two, who had spoken first, smiled warmly at Victoria. 'Yes, we did. Imagine it being so hot the rain evaporates before it hits the ground! I know it's warm in England now, but we never have such amazing weather.'

'This is just the start of the monsoon rains. It's as though someone is tipping a bucket of water over you for about ten minutes then it stops and the sun comes out; this can happen several times a day.'

Nester, the other nurse, looked at Victoria with interest. 'I didn't know you'd been out here before, Victoria. You never said.'

She had nearly revealed her secret. 'I haven't, but I knew someone who worked for an Indian company and they told me all about it.' Satisfied with the explanation the two girls picked up their cutlery and prepared to eat the vegetable stew with steamed rice, which was the lunch menu that day.

Having spoken she now wanted to continue; her tongue was no longer stuck to the roof of her mouth and she was eager to join in the casual talk. 'I'm sorry

I've not been much company for anyone these last few weeks, but the shock of Molly's death...' She stopped, and swallowed. 'The shock of her death was too much. I felt it was my fault.' There, she'd said it out loud, what she had been feeling inside ever since she'd heard the terrible news.

Ann dropped her knife and reached over to grip Victoria's hand. 'You must never think that, Victoria. You did everything you could, so did we all; it was her decision to find somewhere else to shower and it was plain bad luck that she came face to face with an intruder. It was a million-to-one chance; no one is to blame and it's no one's fault.'

'But if someone had checked the shower for her that day, she wouldn't have gone. As you say, her death was a random meeting, but she could have gone the next day and it wouldn't have happened.'

'Well, I suppose there's some logic in that,' Nester said dubiously. 'But, you've got to let it go, Victoria. I've never told you, I was one of the few nurses saved when the ship went down last year. I lost all my friends and in a horrible way. You just have to put it behind you or you'd go mad.'

Victoria blushed. She had been wallowing in self-pity, forgetting there were others who had gone through much worse than her. What was happening?

The nearer she got to her home – only a short stretch of the Indian Ocean separated her from the mainland – the more she reverted to the spoilt girl of her previous life. Even Amelia no longer seemed to be a part of her.

'I'm really sorry. I didn't know. You must all think I'm very weak and self-indulgent. I'm going to try harder, show a little more team spirit. Molly would not want me to grieve for her; I know if I had been the one to die, she would have cried then got on with things.'

Ann released her hand. 'No one blames you for being sad. We all were, and Molly was a special friend of yours. We know that, but I must say I'm delighted you've come back to us now. We've all been so worried about you; you must have lost pounds and look so drawn.'

She glanced round the canteen and met a sea of smiling faces. Her private mourning had been so horribly public. She had to get out of there. Thank God she was back on duty in ten minutes. She dropped her knife and fork back on the plate, half-full of lunch. Pushing her chair back, she half-smiled.

'Thank you so much for your support and kindness. I'm afraid I'm on duty in a minute and I must use the lavatory before I return.'

As she hurried away she wished she hadn't added the unnecessary information about her bodily functions. She hated being the centre of attention, always had, but realised that from now on she would always be viewed with curiosity. Seen as the nurse whose best friend had been murdered, as the nurse who had almost pined away in unnecessary and extravagant grief.

She stopped on the veranda to gain her equilibrium, wondering how she could rectify the situation. There was one thing she could do; she could ask to be transferred. She knew they wanted nurses on the India–Burma front. There was fierce fighting against the Japanese and the hospitals were full – not only of wounded, but with troops with jungle sickness, malaria and dysentery and all the other maladies the Europeans were prone to in her country. Decision made, she hurried back inside to find the captain and put in her request.

Feeling happier than she had for the past four weeks Victoria returned to duty, knowing her request for a transfer had been viewed as a noble sacrifice. She had been promised she would be on the next draft. She continued to work, but was finding it more and more difficult to keep her thoughts away from home – such a short distance, but still out of reach.

She had written a letter to her parents telling them where she was and that she was on her own. She told them Henry had been killed at Dunkirk; she didn't actually lie about Amelia's existence, just didn't mention her and hoped her parents would assume she'd had a miscarriage or stillbirth.

When she finally got her orders to move she would be arriving on the side of India furthest away from her home outside Bombay. If her parents knew it was possible she would be in Madras sometime in the next few weeks, maybe they would take the chance and travel across country in the hope of meeting with her.

The thought of seeing her parents again buoyed her up. She had changed so much, how would her father view his daughter when he saw her in combat uniform? Part of the military operation for a country he must now despise.

Knowing she was eventually going to return eased the waiting. She occasionally went into Colombo with the other girls as a token gesture, but her heart and mind were elsewhere. Nobody could possibly complain she was shirking her duties, but she no longer felt part of the unit.

* * *

The monsoon arrived with a vengeance and she was profoundly grateful for the covered walkway that enabled her to get to her ward without being exposed to the torrential rain. They had all been issued with large umbrellas; she would never forget the strange sight of unknown legs and feet scurrying from place to place.

There was a dramatic increase in jungle fever and infected wounds. The rain was accompanied by blazing sunshine and the constant switch from being soaked to the skin and burnt to a crisp didn't suit most nurses.

However, she revelled in the extremes. She was almost home. She packed her boxes and waited for the summons. Finally her name appeared at the head of a list of a small group of six who were going to Burma. The six consisted of four staff nurses and two sisters. This meant, she was glad to discover, all the arrangements for their travel could be left in the hands of her superiors.

'Victoria, we have to catch the train at dawn. Have you got your boxes ready?' Valerie Dewhurst, the more senior sister, a major by rank, asked.

'They have been packed for the past three weeks. They can be collected any time. What time do I have to report tomorrow morning?'

'An ambulance is taking us at three. Hardly worth going to bed really – the rest of us are going to have a farewell drink with friends in the mess. I hope you're going to join us?'

She intended to refuse then reconsidered. 'Yes, there's no point in going to bed, so why not?'

She collected her tin hat and haversack and joined the other five women in the large recreation hall. She was amazed to see it full of both male and female officers, all smiling and ready to wish her bon voyage. She'd had no idea so many people knew who she was. She only knew a dozen or so names but everyone seemed to know hers.

There was much hilarity and many silly games played that night. Valerie balanced a pint of beer on her head and sang, 'Roll Out the Barrel' to great applause. Others did different party tricks. She watched and laughed and clapped when expected, but felt removed from it all. It was as though she was distancing herself from this part of her life, preparing to start another.

She rested her head against the chair, closing her eyes, allowing her mind to wander. A new life? Why did she think that? She was still a nurse in the QAs, still in the army; she could hardly return to her parents and resume the role of dutiful daughter. To do that she would have to desert and that was something she would never do. Her in-laws and Henry would expect her to remain loyal to the cause she had signed up for.

Really, things would not be much different. She would be amongst familiar people, would understand their native tongues, be on home soil, but she would still be a nurse in the army and answerable to her superiors, unable to move freely or make her own decisions.

She was just travelling from one place to another. Her surroundings would change, but her life would remain essentially the same. However, she had a deep conviction something momentous was going to happen, that being back in India would push her life in a different direction yet again.

* * *

The long train journey from the southern tip of India to Madras was far more interesting than the journey she had made across Africa. The train she and her party were on was a troop train. It was full. There were GIs at one end and these were separated from the British troops by a dozen or so nurses. Both groups sought their attention. Two dozen women, regardless of their shape, size or age were a delightful distraction for these fighting men. They were offered cups of tea and other rations by the British and candy bars and chocolate by the Americans.

Victoria kept herself aloof from all this, remaining quietly in the corner of the compartment, writing in the journal she still kept, or staring pensively out of the window and drinking in the almost familiar sights of this part of India. This was somewhere she'd never visited but understood.

At one stop the rest of the group disembarked to stretch their legs on the station. There was a problem on the line ahead and they would have to wait a couple of hours before they could move. She relished the peace and privacy of being alone for the first time in several days.

She was lost in her own thoughts, praying that somehow her parents would be in Madras waiting to see her. She'd already been told she had five days' leave before she went to the front.

'Excuse me, ma'am, are you unwell?'

She opened her eyes to see an American officer lounging in the open doorway, a worried frown on his handsome face.

Something about this tall, slim man resonated deep inside her. In the four years since Henry's death she'd not noticed other men. But this one was different. There was something about his grey eyes, his quizzical smile, which appealed to her.

'No, I'm not unwell – thank you for asking. I just needed a little time to myself.'

She saw him hesitate, and thought for a moment he would back out and leave and she would not even learn his name. Perhaps he felt the pull between them for, to her surprise, instead of vanishing down the corridor, he came in and sat down on the bench seat opposite.

'I know what you mean – much as I love my buddies – it's great to find a moment to be alone.'

He stretched across the compartment offering his hand. 'Hi, I'm Taylor King, at your service, ma'am.'

Victoria placed her hand in his and saw it disappear. Something similar to an electric shock shot up her arm as his fingers closed. 'I'm pleased to meet you. I'm Victoria Jones.'

He seemed reluctant to release her. She didn't want to remove her hand. For a few moments they remained linked together awkwardly and the tension in the apartment simmered. She snatched her hand back as he released his grip. He leant back in the corner, stretching out his long legs. How strange! She felt the need to reach out again.

'I hadn't realised until I got on this train how many Americans were involved in the war down here.'

'Yes, ma'am. We're helping the Brits hold back the Japs.' They both heard voices in the corridor and he stood up. 'I hope we meet again sometime, ma'am. Do you have furlough in Madras?'

'I do.'

'Then I'll find you and we can have dinner together?'

'That would be lovely.'

The American captain vanished as quietly as he'd arrived, but Victoria had a feeling that she'd see him again. He was the antithesis of Henry. She'd known the moment she opened her eyes and saw him standing in the doorway that he was going to be special to her.

He was taller than Henry and certainly slimmer and his hair was a rich chestnut brown instead of fair. His eyes had mesmerised her. People with auburn hair usually had green or hazel eyes, but his were a peculiar shade of blue and grey. She had no time to dwell on this chance meeting as her fellow travellers bundled back into the compartment.

'Well, Victoria, you didn't miss much. I can't tell

you how indescribably awful the latrines were,' Valerie said, shuddering theatrically.

'I can imagine. It's no coincidence I developed a bladder with an infinite capacity since coming over here. I find I can go hours without needing to use the facilities.' She straightened, giving the returning nurses more room to sit down.

'We saw a very dashing American officer jump down from this carriage. What was he doing in the part of the train that is supposed to be no man's land?'

'Perhaps he was lost?' She shrugged and fiddled with her belt to hide the faint blush spreading over her cheeks.

'He was not lost. I think he was looking for something, or should I say someone?'

All five girls swivelled to stare at her and she grinned. 'You're quite right, he did come in here. I suppose he must have seen me through the window and thought he would try his luck.'

'Go on, tell us all. Did you give him the big heave-ho?' Nester asked eagerly.

For some reason she didn't feel annoyed about this; in fact she was happy to share her excitement. 'Actually, he said he's coming to find me and take me out to dinner when we reach Madras.'

'What's his name then?'

Valerie sounded almost accusatory, as if she'd made it up. 'Captain Taylor King. He was very charming and very attractive.'

'Well, I must say you're a dark horse, Victoria Jones. From what I've heard you've not even batted your eyelids at any of the doctors or officers you've been working with for the past five months and here you are flinging yourself at a complete stranger.'

Her amusement evaporated. 'Valerie, I think you need to get one thing clear. What I do, or don't do, in my private life is absolutely no concern of yours. You're my superior officer and when I'm at work it's different. But what I do in my own time is my own business.'

An uncomfortable silence filled the compartment as the others waited for the explosion. Valerie was known for her fierce temper, and relished her role as a major. Having power over most of the other nurses, as well as all the non-commissioned servicemen, suited her down to the ground.

'Sorry, Victoria. You're quite right; it is none of my business. You deserve a break. You work harder than anyone else and someone you were fond of died in a ghastly way a few weeks ago.'

There was a collective sigh of relief around the

compartment. Victoria's fists unclenched. 'And I'm sorry I was so abrupt. I'm not used to having anyone comment on my social life or lack of it.' She smiled at the women who had almost become friends. 'I've never said, but I was widowed at Dunkirk. I'd only been married two years and I've never looked at another man since. If I'm honest, I've not even noticed that men *were* men, if you know what I mean. It's as much a shock to me that Captain King appealed to me.'

'Good for you, Victoria. A nice night out with a handsome American will do you a power of good. But how on earth is he going to find your address when we don't even know where we're going to be? I've no idea.'

'I'd thought of that, but I'll leave it in the hands of fate. If the captain is sufficiently resourceful, he'll find me. Then I'll know we are meant to be friends.'

17

NEW BEGINNINGS AND OLD PROBLEMS

Victoria stood with the five other nurses at Madras station, beside a mound of baggage. They had been instructed to remain *in situ* until transport could be arranged. This end of the heaving platform was relatively clean and she settled down on her box for the usual long wait.

She listened to the musical chatter and watched the kaleidoscope of colour created by the sari-clad women and breathed in the sweet, exotic smell that was India. She was home at last. Nothing seemed to have change; it was still chaotic. Sacred cows cluttering up the streets, along with people pushing carts laden with produce, women walking with baskets of oranges balanced on their heads, all accompanied by the constant whine of beggars. She thanked God the early monsoon rains they had encountered in Colombo were not drenching this city yet.

In spite of being told to remain where she was she walked away from her friends, trying to adjust to the Hindi and Urdu she could hear, trying to understand what people were saying. She was wrong: things had changed. At least half the crowd were fair-skinned and in military uniform, mostly khaki, but with some of the blue-grey of the air force, and dark blue of the navy, sprinkled amongst them. She was attracting an undue amount of attention. Several servicemen stopped to salute her smartly just for the fun of seeing her return the gesture. Hastily she returned to her group who were so busy exclaiming about the heat, the noise, and the lack of organisation they hadn't noticed her temporary absence.

A harassed junior officer appeared beside them. 'Right, ladies, your chariot awaits. You're being sent to a rather splendid hotel on the outskirts of the city; it's relatively safe and you should get a decent sleep there.'

Victoria was the last to scramble into the rear of the battered truck, which had shuddered to a halt in front of them. How would Captain King, or her parents, find her if she was marooned on the edge of the city?

'Come along, Jones, don't dawdle down there. The sooner we get out of this heat and settled somewhere the better.'

'Yes, Sister, I'm coming.' She leapt nimbly into the back and found herself a space on one of the trunks amongst the pile of luggage. The lorry jerked forward and she clung on to the sides to avoid being catapulted to the floor. Amidst much laughter and high spirits they drove through the city – so familiar but somehow alien.

She felt at home here, but no longer part of it. Her five years living as an Englishwoman meant she no longer belonged in a sari. She could never go back to living in Marpur with her parents even if they wanted her to.

Shrinking back into a corner she closed her eyes. Where did she belong now? Not back in England, it was too cold and grey – she had craved the warmth and colour of India. But now she was here, she had discovered it was no longer where she belonged either. She was a stranger in her own country. Maybe she should not have been so quick to give up her daughter.

Thank God she was a member of the armed

forces because at the moment she had no idea who she was or where she fitted in. Whilst the war was on she had a place in society, a clear role – she was a nursing officer in the QAs.

'Wake up, Victoria. We're here, and it doesn't look half bad.' Nester prodded her sharply on the shoulder.

'I wasn't asleep, just thinking,' she replied with a smile. It's what they all said when they were catching a quick forty winks.

Curiously she looked around to see exactly where she was going to recuperate after the arduous journey. It wasn't as bad as she'd feared; in fact it didn't look a lot different from a seaside hotel in Eastbourne. Not that she'd ever been to the English seaside, but she'd seen pictures in books.

'Come along, everyone, let's get cracking. We seem to be the first. Shall we see if we can get the best rooms?'

There was a chorus of agreement and Valerie led them across the forecourt. They were a motley crew festooned with bags, tin hats and heavy greatcoats. The hotel foyer was a welcome relief after the baking heat outside.

Victoria heard the familiar sound of a creaking ceiling fan and was reminded poignantly of the last time she'd stayed in the Raj Hotel in Bombay on her honeymoon. She trailed along behind the others, indifferent to the clamour for superior accommodation. What she wanted to know was the name of this establishment, its exact location, and if there was a telephone she could use.

Valerie turned, three keys held triumphantly aloft. 'Look, we only have two to a room. The rest of them are four to a room. We're on the first floor at the back and we have a view of the gardens.'

'Where's our luggage gone? The lorry that brought us has vanished and I can't see our boxes anywhere,' Nester wailed. 'If they've gone off with them, we'll be put on a charge.'

'Don't panic, the boxes were unloaded and they've been taken upstairs. I think we'll find them waiting by our rooms.' Victoria had watched the Indian porters carry them inside.

'How in God's name do they know which rooms we were going to be allocated? Or who is sleeping with whom?' Valerie didn't like anyone else being in possession of information she didn't have.

'Shall we go upstairs and see?' Victoria suggested tactfully.

They clanked and rattled up the wide marble stairs into the spacious upper hallway. Sure enough, as she had predicted, their boxes were stacked neatly on the floor. Standing in front of them were three uniformed porters, all Indian, smiling happily, waiting to be told where to dispose of the belongings.

Valerie strode along to the first room and unlocked the door with a flourish. 'Well, this one looks excellent. Nester and I will have this. Here, Victoria and Enid you go next door, and that leaves the third one for Ann and Betty.'

Obediently Victoria stepped forward and taking the proffered key handed it over to Enid. She wasn't as eager to see inside as the others. She knew what she would find: a large airy room with beds and mosquito nets, and acres of cool marble floor to walk on.

'Look at this, Victoria, it's smashing.'

She followed Enid into the room. There were two giant double beds so she wouldn't have to share and push a bolster down the middle. 'Yes, it's wonderful. Absolute luxury after the places we've had to sleep in over the last six months. Have you looked at the bathroom?'

Enid dropped her belongings with a clatter and rushed to open the door. 'My word! Fit for a king in here. And to think, you can have a bath every day and don't have to worry about how much water you use.'

'I don't think water is going to be a problem, the

monsoon is about to arrive; there will soon be more than enough of the wretched stuff.'

Her friend emerged grinning happily. 'Well, I'm going to have a bath straightaway. We've been cooped up on the train so long I stink to high heaven.'

'We all do. You go ahead.' There was a knock on the exterior door. 'These must be boxes coming in now.' She walked across to open it and one of the smiling porters staggered in with the first box. 'Thank you; please put them over by the wall, if you would. I don't think we'll be unpacking the boxes as we're only here for a week.'

'Yes, madam, very good, madam.' The man bowed then realising his error hastily saluted as well. He backed out as if leaving royalty, a second sharp reminder of her previous status. She had to restrain herself from responding as she used to at home.

Whilst her room-mate was in the bathroom she quickly unpacked her holdall and haversack, then unearthed her washbag and makeup. She needed a complete change of clothes, but as all they were allowed to wear was their uniform, she didn't have to waste time selecting. She found the cloth bag for putting laundry in and shoved her dirty things inside. She waited in her dressing gown for her turn to get clean.

When she emerged from the bathroom Enid had disappeared, presumably to join the others downstairs. She enjoyed the privacy, a rare commodity nowadays. She stood in front of the speckled full-length mirror. She was too thin, but luckily her breasts were still firm and her waist tiny. She had been lucky to have very few stretch marks from her pregnancy. She stepped closer to the mirror, staring hard, trying to decide if someone who didn't know she had had a baby would be able to tell from looking. She was examining her breasts when she froze. What on earth was she doing? Why should she be worried about what she looked like naked?

Heat travelled from her toes to her crown and she shivered, clutching her arms around her. Meeting Taylor King had unlocked the door she had been hiding behind for the past five years. Her breasts hardened beneath her fingers as she thought about the American she'd met for scarcely ten minutes.

It had only taken that long to know Henry was the man for her. Had she, for the second time, fallen for a stranger – only this time he was American not English? Was it fate taking a hand once more? After all, hadn't she met both Henry and Taylor King on a train?

Well, time would tell. This time she was not a shy

seventeen-year-old virgin with no experience. She recognised her feelings for what they were: sexual desire. Her brief relationship with Henry had taught her how powerful this was, perhaps even stronger than an emotional connection.

She pulled on her regulation underwear and slightly creased fresh uniform. Five minutes later she was locking the bedroom door and on her way downstairs in search of the information she needed if she was to attempt to contact her parents and let them know where she was staying. She rather hoped they would remember to enquire for Nurse Jones. Well, First Lieutenant Jones would be more correct.

The babble of voices rose from the foyer; the other residents had obviously arrived and were waiting to be directed to their rooms. She met several smiling Indian porters carrying baggage and nodded as she went past. They were lucky to have arrived before this crush and to have secured the three best rooms in the place.

She stopped at the foot of the stairs and surveyed the confusion. There was no point in approaching the reception desk at the moment, she would go outside and have a look round. She could hardly assimilate the fact she was finally, after five long years, back in India.

Outside the chaos was almost as bad. Stinking trucks and other vehicles were reversing and turning, making it impossible to cross the forecourt safely. Some were dropping off yet more guests, others returning from whence they came. Sick of being forced to salute every time she met a member of the ranks she went to look for her friends. She had seen no sign of them as she'd come down; surely they hadn't gone back into Madras?

'Victoria. Victoria, we're over here.'

Valerie was calling from somewhere. But where? She scanned the windows on the ground floor and finally spotted the caller waving from behind the balustrade of a grand veranda. Of course, they'd found the bar.

She ran across, dodging the soldiers and porters, and found a set of steps that led to where the women were waiting.

'I might have known you'd all be here; isn't it a little early for alcohol?'

'It's never too early and anyway, it's been a long and tiring day. I think we're entitled to relax; after all we're on leave aren't we?' Valerie patted the empty chair beside her and Victoria dropped onto it.

'It's bedlam inside. We did well to be unpacked and out here before everyone else arrived. Does anyone know exactly where we are, what this place is called?'

'It's called the Indian Heritage Hotel, and I even have the full address and phone number for you.' Enid waved a slip of paper triumphantly.

'Thank you so much. Friends of my uncle, you know the one who worked for the Indian company, live in Madras. I was hoping I might catch up with them.'

'A likely story. You want to be sure your handsome Yank finds you, and I don't blame you. I wish someone like him would come looking for me,' Nester said.

The six of them drank gin and tonics with gusto and by the time the dining room opened they hardly cared what they ate. Victoria persuaded them to be more adventurous with their choices and was delighted that they all enjoyed their meal. With every mouthful of the spicy aromatic vegetable stew she swallowed she became more Indian.

When they eventually staggered back to their rooms the foyer was quiet and they were able to regain their bedrooms without being obliged to salute a dozen grinning privates.

The next morning she rose early and left Enid sleeping soundly. She wanted to try and ring her parents whilst there was no danger of being overheard. Downstairs there was an unknown receptionist rubbing his eyes behind the impressive desk. He had obviously just completed the night shift.

'Good morning, I wonder if it would be possible to use your telephone?'

The man swallowed his yawn and fixed a polite smile on his face. 'Of course, ma'am. If you would care to wait in that booth over there, I will try and connect you. Do you have the telephone number you wish to contact?'

She wrote down the number of her home and hurried across to the small cubicle. She pulled out the chair and sat watching the telephone, willing it to ring. When the shrill tones echoed round her cubicle she was unable to reach over and pick up the receiver. She had to force herself to move.

'Hello?'

There were crackles and hisses and then she heard the voice she'd been dreaming about for the last five years. 'Victoria? Is that you, my darling?'

Tears spilled down her cheeks and she was unable to answer. 'Yes, Mama, it is. I can hardly believe I'm talking to you. I'm staying at a hotel called the Indian Heritage. It's on the outskirts of Madras. I have another six days' leave before being transferred to the front line. Is it possible you and Papa can get down here to see me?'

This time it was her father who spoke. 'We could hardly believe it when we got your letter, my dear. After all these years, to know you are alive and well and back in India. We are ready to leave; we have just been waiting for your call. It will take us two days to get to Madras by train, but we will be there, I promise you.'

'How are you both? How are things here? I've been reading about the violence, the anti-British feeling, but I've noticed no resentment since I got back.'

'It's the war, my dear girl. Most people realise that being invaded by Japan would be far worse than being occupied by Britain. But as soon as it's over, independence will come. The politicians have almost everything arranged. But let's not talk about that; tell me how you come to be a nurse and a lieutenant in the British Army.'

Victoria talked to her parents for over an hour. She learnt her father had been transferring his money into portable stocks, and her home in Marpur was about to be sold to developers. It was prime real estate; the demand from Bombay's new businesses and the ever-growing number of inhabitants meant he had got a premium price for the land.

They intended to move to Delhi as her father had business interests there. Here they would become plain Mr and Mrs Bahani, leave the title and principality behind. They had asked about Henry's death, and her mother had asked about the pregnancy. She had been forced to lie, yet again, and told her mother she had had a miscarriage. Denying Amelia's existence had been the hardest thing. She was their granddaughter, and they deserved to know everything about her. But she'd made her decision last year. Far better if her daughter remained with Marion and Arthur.

Slowly she replaced the receiver and stood up. God knows how much the call had cost, but it was worth every rupee. Dizzy with happiness she walked out into the sunshine, planning how she would explain the arrival of her aristocratic Indian father and sari-clad English mother. She'd told them she had invented an uncle and that they were to be his mythical friends come to see her.

They understood perfectly. After all they had told her, when she'd made her decision to marry Henry so long ago, she would have to remain in the world she had chosen. Although she was meeting her parents, she would be able to talk to them freely and would still be drowning in secrets.

18

REUNION

Enid was dressed and ready for breakfast when Victoria returned to her room. 'Golly, you're an early bird, Victoria. You must have been up at first light.'

'I was. To tell you the truth, I'm getting rather tired of being saluted and I wanted to explore before anyone else was up. Judging by the racket going past our room last night we were not the only ones to indulge in the bar.'

'Valerie said other ranks aren't staying here; it's only for officers. The non-commissioned lot will have been shunted off elsewhere. With any luck we will have the place to ourselves from now on. There are sufficient Indian porters around to do anything that needs doing.'

'I certainly didn't see any just now, but then the only people up were staff.'

They ambled along to the dining room where the other four were already tucking into a hearty breakfast.

'What are you going to do today? Betty, Ann, Nester and I are going to spend the day lazing around the hotel,' Valerie said as she wiped the last morsel of egg from her plate.

'The same as you, I think, Valerie. What about you, Enid? Do you want to do anything energetic?'

'No fear. The whole point of having leave is to put your feet up, not traipse around the place. And anyway, I heard an Indian chappie saying the first real monsoon rains are expected today. The last thing I want is to get soaked to the skin. We've had more than enough of that already in Colombo.'

The unaccustomed inactivity began to pall by mid-afternoon and even the imminent arrival off torrential rain didn't deter Victoria from heading off into the gardens for a brisk walk. The other five declined. They'd already joined with another group of nurses who were just back from the front.

She didn't really want to hear how awful it was there, how much the girls had hated it; she was fully aware of the dangers and disadvantages, but as long as she was in India she didn't care what she did. She prayed she wouldn't be posted back to England before the end of the war. She intended to apply for her discharge papers and quietly slip away; Nurse Jones would vanish forever, to be replaced by Miss Bahani, the unmarried daughter of the wealthy Bahanis of Delhi.

Talk was that things were going well in Europe since the Yanks had joined in. Hitler was being pushed back on all fronts, Mussolini had surrendered the previous summer. Only the Japanese were fighting fiercely. What she knew of this race was they never gave in; surrender was not an option.

She ran down the front steps, glad the threat of rain had driven everyone else inside and the large forecourt was quiet. She paused, trying to decide in which direction to go. She heard a vehicle approaching fast; it didn't sound like the rackety engine of a British transport, it sounded more like an American Jeep. A frisson of excitement ran down her spine.

Victoria waited under the portico to see if Captain King had come to seek her out. The vehicle screeched to a halt in front of her.

'Excuse me, ma'am, is this the Indian Heritage

Hotel?' The young GI saluted smartly and waited for her reply.

She hid her disappointment. 'Yes, it is. If you go through the main door you'll find someone at reception who will be able to help you.'

The young man grinned, making him look little more than a boy. 'I reckon I've found the lady I want to see, ma'am. Are you, by any chance, Lieutenant Jones?'

'I am. The only American I know is Captain King. Are you by any chance a messenger from him?'

'Sure am, Lieutenant Jones. Captain King sends his apologies, but his leave's been cancelled. He asked me to give you this letter.'

She walked up to the Jeep and held out her hand. The letter was surprisingly thick. Taylor had obviously written more than a *Dear John*.

'That's not all, ma'am – there's a real pretty box of candy for you too.' The GI dived under his seat and removed an embarrassingly large, beribboned box and handed it to her.

'Thank you, and please thank Captain King.'

The young man saluted again and with a squeal of rubber shot off just as the heavens opened and the monsoon began. Victoria, well used to taking evasive action, was back inside before her precious box of chocolates had been ruined by the rain. She tucked the satisfyingly thick letter into her battledress pocket for later and headed to the bar to share the unexpected bounty with her friends.

* * *

After dinner she made her apologies and slipped away, claiming she had a headache. She saw the others exchange knowing glances. They must think she was suffering because her American had not been able to come and see her. She had been receiving sympathetic glances all evening.

Scrambling onto her bed, she dropped the mosquito net around before removing the envelope from her pocket. History was repeating itself. Sitting cocooned by the billowing whiteness, her precious letter in her hand, reminded her of the time Henry had thrown his message over her veranda the night he'd arrived at Marpur.

She smiled at the memory – the circumstances were similar, but she was a different person now. After ripping open the envelope she removed the wad of paper and flattened it. As she read she felt as though Taylor was there beside her; he knew how to write a letter that went straight to the heart.

He explained how bad he felt about being sent away, about not being able to make their date. He said he'd been bowled over by her, and that he couldn't stop thinking about her. He begged her forgiveness and promised as soon as he got any leave he'd come and find her, front line or not. She should expect a visit from him any day soon. She was intrigued by the biographical details – it seemed that, like Henry, Taylor was the only son of one of the premier families in Boston. There were two older sisters, both married with children, but he was heir to the properties and estates.

She folded the five pages carefully and pushed them back into the envelope. Why had he felt it necessary to explain his background, make a point of saying how wealthy he was? The most likely explanation was he'd felt the instant rapport that she had. Well, she wasn't going to worry about it at the moment. She had far more important things on her mind. Her parents were arriving the next day and because they wouldn't be able to stay at the Indian Heritage, she was going to go with them and spend the rest of her leave in Madras. No doubt there was a Raj Hotel here, and her father would have reserved a suite, as he always did when he travelled.

She had already told her friends she was going

away and they were pleased she had something to take her mind off the missing Captain King. When Enid stumbled in, in the small hours, humming a bawdy song none too quietly, she feigned sleep. She had no wish to share her thoughts with a slightly tipsy young woman she'd known for barely a week.

The rain turned off like a tap the following morning and the sun shone with unrelenting bright-ness. The vegetation steamed gently and the residents of the hotel jumped nimbly from dry spot to dry spot. Her backpack and holdall were packed, she'd signed out and put her address for the next four nights as the Raj Hotel. Although she was on leave, she was not allowed to go anywhere without supplying her whereabouts.

She'd said her farewells to Enid and the others and left them in the bar playing bridge with the nurses from the front. Impatiently, she marched up and down the portico, willing a taxi to come, bringing her beloved parents with it.

Eventually she got sick of being saluted by the drivers waiting to collect officers whose leave was over, and went back inside to wait in the entrance hall. She was chatting to the concierge with her back to the doors and didn't see her parents arrive.

'Victoria, is that you?'

She spun round, hanging on to the edge of the counter to stop herself from flinging her arms around her mother. They stood facing each other. The air shimmered with emotion. Victoria smiled, and this was enough. Her mother looked thinner, but no different really, more Indian perhaps, more comfortable in the traditional sari than she had been that last night she'd seen her.

She raised her eyes to her father, drinking in his glittering eyes and lips pressed hard together to avoid their trembling. He now had two wings of white on either side of his temples, making him look more distinguished, if that was possible. He was wearing his usual black, high-collared jacket and trousers, the traditional dress of a Brahmin, and he exuded wealth and power.

'Excuse me, sir, but this hotel is for military personnel only. I'm afraid there are no vacancies for civilians.'

Her father impaled the young man behind the counter with his aristocratic stare and she watched him collapse and almost back away.

'Thank you. We have come to collect a young friend of ours. We have no intention of staying here; we have our usual suite at the Raj.'

He turned his back and strode off. She fell in beside her mother, just as she had always done, and followed him outside to the waiting taxi. Papa sat in the front, next to the driver, and she and her mother sat stiffly on the back seat. Things were awkward. Even away from the prying eyes of people who knew her she didn't dare to speak freely. She was supposed to be a British nurse. Why would she wish to embrace Indians?

She inhaled the distinctive smell of her parents; she had forgotten about the lemony pomade her father put on his thick hair and the sweet, rose-scented toilet water her mother habitually used. Now she closed her eyes and revelled in the familiar scents feeling the years trickle away, until she was Victoria Bahani and the intervening years were as nothing.

The taxi rattled down an imposing drive and pulled up smoothly outside the hotel. Two doormen, in familiar red turbans and smart white outfits, stepped forward and opened the door, bowing them into the hotel. Her father didn't pause to collect a key, but continued up the staircase and along to the rear of the hotel where, as expected, he'd managed to reserve a small suite of rooms. Not quite the luxury he enjoyed in Delhi, but more than adequate, even for a rajah.

The door closed and finally she was alone with

her parents. Victoria flung herself into her mother's arms and as they closed her usually reserved father added his strong hold. They stood, the three of them, swaying, crying, as the pain of the past five years washed away.

'I think that will do, my dears. I have ordered refreshments to be sent up. It wouldn't be appropriate to be discovered embracing like this.'

Victoria felt a crisp linen handkerchief being pressed into her fingers and she mopped her eyes and blew her nose loudly. 'I can't believe I'm standing here, so close to you. I honestly thought when I left five years ago that I'd never see you again. If Henry had lived, I never would have, so some good came out of that disaster after all.'

'Do you know, my darling, I believe you've grown a little. I suppose at seventeen that's not unusual. See, you're a good two inches taller than me.' Her mother slipped her arm around her waist and they walked across the luxurious reception room to sit, side by side, on the maroon silk sofa.

'It seems so strange, being back in India. I remember you told me I couldn't live in both worlds and I think you're right. The awful thing is I don't belong in England, and now I fear I don't belong here either.'

There was a tentative knock on the door and her father's reply was postponed whilst the two waiters wheeled in the laden trolleys. They set the feast out on a pristine damask cloth and then, bowing, retreated – obviously knowing they were not needed to serve. What they made of the strange trio she had no idea. She no longer looked Indian. Her face was tanned, her hair shorter, worn in a neat roll at the back of her neck. Her battledress and beret made her look as English as the next Q A.

'Are you hungry, Victoria darling? We have ordered all the things you used to love. It must have been so hard for you being forced to eat meat. English food is awful; they have no idea how to cook and prepare anything.'

Over a sumptuous lunch Victoria told them everything that had happened to her, apart from the one omission: Amelia's existence. This deception marred what should have been a perfect moment. Before long it was as though she had never been away. Her imminent departure to the battlefront wasn't discussed.

It was her father later on that day who broached the delicate subject of how their lives might be in the future. 'Victoria, my darling girl, it is good to see you so well, but you are far too thin. Now, both of you, sit down. There are serious issues we need to discuss. Although Victoria has officially got four more nights' leave, we all know she could be called back at any time.'

He waited until they were comfortable on the sofa then pulled over a curved-back chair and sat facing them. 'As I told you on the telephone two days ago, Victoria, I have sold our home and the estates. The money has been transferred to my account in Delhi; I have been turning some of my assets into diamonds, so much easier to carry. I have also increased your trust fund; you'll find that whatever happens in the future, you will never have to go without.'

'I don't care about the money; what I want to know is how we're going to be together here after the war.'

'I don't think we can, my darling. You have no choice, you must return to Britain and continue in your life as a nurse. It seems we shall be offered British passports, and your mother and I intend to follow you to England as soon as it is practical. Once there, I shall buy a property and then you will be able to join us whenever you wish.'

'I know it's not what you want to hear, Victoria, but you must understand. We have to be so careful at the moment. If anyone suspected your ancestry it would make life difficult for all of us. Your father is a respected businessman. In the current atmosphere he would be ostracised, maybe ruined, if word got out our daughter was a member of the British Armed Forces.'

She squeezed her mother's hand. 'I understand, Mama. I think I already knew how things would be. We have managed to survive apart for five years. This wretched conflict cannot go on for much longer. In fact people are talking about it being over in Europe by next year.'

'But not over here, my dear. The Japanese are a tenacious race; I have often done business with them in the past. They would rather commit hara-kiri than surrender. The war on the Burma front could go on for years and whilst you're still needed, whatever the situation in Europe, the Minister of War will not let you go. You had better resign yourself to being in India for the foreseeable future, but I doubt if we will be able to meet again like this.'

She sat back, looking from one to the other, wondering when they had become so negative. Couldn't they see just being in India was enough for her at the moment? They could phone each other, write letters, and even if she was working on the front she would get occasional leave.

'I belong here. Staying in India is fine by me. Whatever you say, I'm sure things are not as bleak as they look.'

Victoria spent the remainder of the day cooped up in the rooms. She couldn't be seen out with her parents without causing comment. That night as she lay sleepless, listening to the creaking overhead fan in the small side room more normally used for accompanying servants, she tried to analyse how she felt about seeing her parents again after five years.

She smiled as she remembered the way she and her mother had automatically walked behind her father as they'd left the Indian Heritage that morning. Superficially it seemed nothing had changed, that she was still very much a dutiful daughter and he the imperious rajah.

Over the evening she realised her father was treating her as an equal, and her mother appeared to be slightly in awe of her. She had experienced so much, seen things she'd rather not have seen, over the past few years. Her understanding of the war, and the world, was far greater than either of her parents.

Could she ever go back to living with them, whether in England or elsewhere? She didn't hesitate; she knew the answer was no. She had moved on, grown up, was an independent, highly qualified member of a medical team. Even when the war was over she did not intend to give up nursing. It was her forte. She was good at it.

Papa had been right – she couldn't stay in India. She would have to go back to little, chilly England and eat the indescribably awful food again. Her heart quickened – at least then she would be on the same continent as Amelia. The country would be in tatters by the end of the war. There had been so much bomb damage, so many shortages, and her skills would be needed. She could hardly believe how much the Americans had – what a contrast!

As she drifted off to sleep she wondered if her future perhaps might not be in England. Could Taylor's letter, which she had reread several times, be suggesting she go to America? It was clear the message he'd wished to send was that he'd felt the same attraction. All the details about his family were his way of telling her that his intentions were honourable.

Why were all the men in her life wealthy? Henry had been a serving soldier, but when the war was over he would have been like his father, living solely to please himself on inherited money. Taylor came from a similar background; it was obvious from his letter his family were top-drawer, the equivalent of the aristocracy in that part of America.

She sat up. She was wide awake and the irritating clicks of the fan, rather than being comforting, were now a downright annoyance. She pushed aside the mosquito net and ran across to the switch; after three attempts she found the correct one and the noise stopped. She checked the window was firmly closed as she didn't want to share her room with a swarm of mosquitoes.

Suddenly her bedside telephone rang, making her drop the book she was attempting to read. She reached over and picked it up.

'Lieutenant Jones speaking.'

'Lieutenant Jones, they want you to report at Madras station at six o'clock this morning. It seems your draft has been recalled.'

19

FLIGHT TO THE JUNGLE

Victoria thought for a moment. 'I would like to have a taxi waiting outside in twenty minutes. I know it's the middle of the night, but I have to get back to the Indian Heritage or my kit might well be left behind.'

'No problem at all, madam.'

She dressed quickly. After ramming her belongings back into her bag she hurried across reception to the room occupied by her parents. She paused; she'd never been in their bedroom when they were actually in bed together. This just wasn't done, but if she wanted to say goodbye to them, and she did, she'd have to break the unwritten rule.

She knocked more loudly than she'd intended and then waited, but heard no sound of movement.

She banged more loudly and then cautiously opened the door, and poking her head around, she whispered, 'I'm really sorry to disturb you, but I've got to go in ten minutes.'

The larger of the shrouded shapes behind the mosquito net sat up. 'Give us a moment, my dear, and we will be with you.'

She closed the door and paced anxiously, one eye on the clock, the other watching the door. She'd never known either of her parents to appear in their nightwear; they always left their rooms fully clothed. She didn't have long to wait. The door opened almost immediately and they emerged dressed discreetly in matching silk dressing gowns. Her mother's long hair was neatly braided and hanging down her back, her father's in perfect order, not a strand out of place. How did they manage to look so immaculate even in the middle of the night?

'Thank you for getting up. There's a flap on somewhere and my unit has been recalled. I have to report to the station at six o'clock this morning, but as my stuff is back at the Indian Heritage I must go there first. The others might bring my boxes, but if you don't sit on them yourself they can vanish.'

Her father chuckled. 'How very true, my dear. Well, at least we had one day together, one day more than any of us ever expected. You have our new address and telephone number. If you get time, contact us. We might not be able to get out and see you, but at least we will know that you're well.'

Her mother was too upset to speak. They embraced and her father patted her on the shoulder.

'I must go; I have a taxi waiting. I love you. Take care of yourselves.' She rushed from the room, praying it would not be another five years before she saw them again.

She ran through the deserted hotel, jumped into the waiting taxi, and slammed the door. The vehicle roared off, throwing her violently across the slippery seat. The night was inky black, no street lights anywhere, and the car swerved from side to side to avoid the potholes, its feeble headlights barely adequate. She was relieved when she arrived back at her hotel in one piece.

As the car juddered to a halt, she reached into her bag to pay. 'Thank you, madam, it's all taken care of. Good luck.' The driver barely waited for her to descend before revving noisily and vanishing into the darkness.

This hotel was certainly not deserted. Victoria could see they were obviously not the only group to be recalled. She ran through the foyer, dodging round the boxes and waiting officers and continued upstairs. She knocked on the door and without waiting for a reply from Enid went in.

'Thank goodness! We hoped you'd get back; we had no idea whether to take your boxes with us or leave them here and hope you came to collect them for yourself.'

'Well, I'm here now, thanks. Have you any idea where we're going, or why we've been sent for in such a hurry?'

Enid shook her head. 'Not the foggiest. We knew something was up as there's been a lot of serious faces on the high-ups all day. No doubt we'll be informed in good time.'

Victoria barely had time to use the bathroom before an ever-smiling Indian porter appeared to carry their boxes down. She and Enid followed them and as soon as they were put outside under the portico, they sat down, making sure no one else went away with their belongings.

'Oh, there you are, Victoria. It's a shame you had such a short time with your friends, but a good thing you managed to get back.'

Valerie was back in authoritarian mode and Victoria was happy to sit back and let her organise things. Twenty minutes later the same beaten-up old lorry arrived to collect them, but this time there were twelve nurses to squash in, as well as all the extra paraphernalia.

'Thank God this lorry has a canvas roof of sorts. I've had quite enough of sitting around soaked to the skin.' Nester was always the first to criticise or comment.

Somehow they jammed themselves inside the restricted space and, holding on to any available pro-tuberance, they were bounced and jounced back to Madras station. She was surprised to discover the train already there. Again they were forced to put twelve people and their belongings into a space nor-mally used by six. By using the boxes as seats they fitted in eventually.

'None of us has had any sleep tonight, so I suggest those sitting on the seats get some shut-eye first. We'll change over in two hours, if we're not forced to move before then,' Valerie suggested. They all agreed this was a fair arrangement. Victoria was far too tired to argue; she could sleep quite happily propped as she was against the door.

* * *

The tedious train journey took three days. There were no dining cars or refreshments available. Every time the train stopped at a halt or station someone had to jump off and buy food from the vendors crouched on the platforms and bring it back, balanced on banana leaves, for the others.

Victoria and Enid volunteered for this duty. Although she couldn't use her Hindi or Urdu she was able to understand what was being sold and how much it cost. They now knew their first destination was to be Calcutta. Every time the train halted more American and English service personnel piled on. Only twelve to a compartment now seemed positively spacious.

The platform at Calcutta was chaos; troops looking for their officers, GIs looking for their packs, and nurses guarding their precious boxes.

'You lot wait here; someone sit on my box for me. I'm going to see where we're headed, find some porters and see if there's transport.' Valerie strode off, a militant light in her eyes.

Exhausted and dispirited, the group collapsed like so many rag dolls. Victoria ignored the ribald comments from the soldiers and suggestive remarks from the GIs. She was too tired and dirty to respond.

'I can hardly believe these men still have the energy or inclination to flirt. Look at us, hardly attractive, now are we?' Enid said.

Ann laughed, she was the belle of the bunch, with golden curls and bright blue eyes. 'Speak for yourself, Enid. I think sweat is the new fragrance this year.'

Victoria, who was sitting on two boxes stacked one on top of the other, saw their leader returning. She didn't look pleased.

'Well, ladies, I've got good news and bad. The good news is that there appears to be transport laid on for us, and porters are on their way to collect our luggage. The bad is that it's taking us to the transit camp and nobody knows where to after that.'

'Not to worry – all I want is to get a shower and something to eat and flake out for a few hours,' Enid said.

'Then up you get, everyone. The sooner we move the sooner we will get there.'

Stating the obvious was a feature of Valerie's conversation and usually Victoria responded with a truism of her own, but she was too exhausted to do more than follow orders. She trooped after the porters, never letting her precious baggage out of sight, and arrived outside the station where the truck was waiting.

A loud altercation could be heard over the general hubbub. Men's voices were raised in anger and they soon discovered it was their truck that was the centre of the argument.

A red-faced, sweating infantry officer was attempting to load his troops and their bags on board, but a row of Indian soldiers stood guard around it, refusing to budge and ignoring the commands to move.

'Oh God! What do we do now?' Nester whispered to Valerie.

'We get on the bloody truck, you halfwit. What do you think we should do? Let the bloody men take it and leave us stranded here for the night?'

The wall of smiling Indian guards parted sufficiently to allow them to slip through. Victoria could feel the animosity from the assembled men. They stepped aside muttering obscenities and the truck shot off, taking them God knows where.

This was not an auspicious start. She had believed nurses were welcome wherever they went and always treated with respect. She had just learnt the hard way that when it came to transport it was every soldier for himself; women and children first did not exist out here.

She tried to summon up some enthusiasm for her

surroundings. Hadn't she been dreaming for five years of seeing her homeland again? She was tired and miserable and no more 'at home' here than her compatriots. The people she saw were like skeletons, huge sunken eyes peering listlessly out of skull-like faces. Calcutta was in the midst of a famine and there was nothing she, or any of the well-fed soldiers, could do about it. War Office priorities were to keep the Japanese out of India at all costs. No money or resources could be spared to feed the millions of starving civilians.

The lorry pulled up outside Camp 92 and two soldiers stepped forward, waving their guns. The corporal shouted up at Valerie. 'Who the hell are you? We've not been told that any nurses are arriving today.'

'That's as may be, Corporal, but you will unlock the gate and allow us to enter. Do you want to be reported for disobeying a direct order?' With bad grace the men stepped back and conferred out of earshot.

'Shall we get down? It will be much harder to turn us away if we're standing in front of them. After all we're the officers here.' Victoria had had enough of the uncomfortable lorry and before the others could protest she jumped over the tailgate and was standing, every inch an officer, glaring at the two men.

'The lorry can't go in, ma'am. It will get stuck; it's like a mudbath in there.'

'Fine. We'll unload our belongings and get the porters to carry them to our quarters.'

She could hear the rest of the group climbing down. 'Open the gates. Our CO will take command of things now.'

Valerie soon had the boxes and bags safely inside the gates and the lorry drove away at speed, covering the two sentries with mud. Their profanities were like music to Victoria's ears.

Ann was designated to be in charge of guarding their belongings and three of the newer arrivals plonked themselves firmly across the pile, glaring at anyone who came within arm's reach. The rest of them fell in behind Valerie and went in search of Matron's quarters. They were forced to jump stagnant pools of water left from the previous day's rain; the general dilapidation of the place added to their discomfort.

Matron was a formidable woman, making even Valerie seem benign. They stood to attention and saluted smartly. Victoria felt decidedly silly in her filthy clothes and lopsided beret, but the camp commander was the kind of woman who demanded that sort of respect.

'You are late; you were on my chit for yesterday. The sisters' mess is ready for your use. Get yourselves cleaned up, change into fresh uniforms and be ready to leave at first light tomorrow. I shall inform the wing commander his party of nurses is ready for dispatch.'

Victoria saluted smartly. 'Yes, ma'am.' They spun round and quick-marched out.

'Wonder where the sisters' mess is, Valerie? I know this place is a transit camp for medical staff, but you'd think they'd tidy it up a bit. And they could put signs on the end of the rows so a person can find their way around.'

'We've tongues in our heads, Nester. I shall ask – someone's bound to know.'

It appeared there had been few nursing sisters passing through this particular camp and nobody knew the whereabouts of their accommodation. Eventually a friendly RTO led them to the building.

'You'll find everything tickety-boo in here, ladies. Hot water, rations and beds. Your bedrolls and so on should be here any moment.'

He handed Valerie the key and vanished into the gloom, leaving them to look after themselves. As promised the Indian porters trotted in with their parcels, Ann and the other girls panting behind them.

'This isn't so bad, is it?' Ann said as she came in. 'Plenty of room and enough camp beds to go round.'

'They knew twelve of us were coming. They might be stupid but they can count,' Valerie snapped.

She could envisage a full-scale row blowing up so hastily intervened. 'Thank God we're not in one of those tents tonight. Can you hear? The rain's started. We had better make the most of this. I expect it will be the last fixed structure we sleep in for a long time. It's all tents in the jungle.'

Enid understood. 'I don't mind about tents; in fact I'd rather sleep in a tent than the horrid little cubicles we had in Africa. It's the flight I'm not looking forward to.' Victoria had been about to reassure her, reveal that she'd travelled from India to England five years before in a plane, but luckily remembered in time. 'It's against nature, a huge hunk of metal up in the sky like that.'

Amidst the general chorus of laughter and agreement the bad feeling was forgotten. It rained heavily in the night, and if the compound had been unpleasant before, now it was a quagmire. They had not needed to venture out to find a canteen; the rations provided were more than adequate. There was a Primus stove to make tea and condensed milk to put in it. Victoria had developed a liking for this strange mix.

She woke refreshed and raring to go; there was nothing like a clean uniform, a good sleep and a hearty breakfast to restore one's spirits. She adjusted her beret to a jaunty angle and was ready when there was a loud hammering on the door. Betty was nearest and opened it to find the wing commander, a scruffy-looking individual in a uniform that looked as though it was meant for someone two sizes bigger.

'Good morning, ladies. Your transport awaits.' He looked round the room at the modest pile of luggage. 'Good, my old crate would fall apart at the seams if I put much more in.' He gestured over his shoulder and a different group of Indian soldiers came in to collect the boxes.

'Follow me, ladies, there's a lorry waiting at the gates. If I brought it in, it would have flooded the tents as it went past. Sorry, you're going to have to walk.'

Not sure why he was apologising, Victoria slung her tin hat and greatcoat over her shoulder and was the first to step out into a nightmare scene.

'Good God! We need gumboots to get through

this.' It was hard to distinguish paths from puddles, but the wing co strode off as if it was a clean concrete path in a barracks back in England.

'Nothing for it, girls, unless someone's volunteering to give us a piggyback?' Valerie, pleased with her joke, chuckled loudly and they all managed a dutiful smile.

By taking a circuitous route around the tents and permanent structures they arrived at the exit gate with mud only up to the knees. Their luggage was already piled in the lorry and all they had to do was scramble in on top of it.

They arrived at the airfield far too soon and Victoria, on viewing their transport, regretted having eaten a large breakfast. The dilapidated aeroplane waiting to transport them into the jungle was nothing like the shiny silver monster she'd travelled in from Bombay to England.

Porters tossed their boxes in through the doors and reluctantly she followed. The interior of the plane was piled high, almost to the ceiling, with luggage and other goods. The sergeant instructed them to try and get comfortable on the pile of freight. He added ominously, 'Here, you'll need this. It gets a bit bumpy up there. And you'll need to keep your greatcoats handy as it also gets cold.'

She knew what the paper was for and shuddered. There were a couple of spaces between the boxes in which to push her feet; next she spread her greatcoat out beside her, and used her holdall for a pillow. The newspaper she left in her lap.

Two RAF men crawled over the baggage and lay one on each side of the plane, stretched out on a narrow metal sill alongside a row of tiny windows. She realised they were spotters, there to look out for Japanese planes. What good that would do she had no idea, as their plane was too old and cumbersome to manoeuvre out of the way. She prayed Spitfires would be giving them air cover.

They took off and at once she felt the all too familiar nausea. By the end of a long flight she was grateful for the pile of newspaper and was longing for deliverance. She fell out of the plane glad to dispose of her well-used newspaper parcel in the nearest bin, watching the others do the same. They waited for the coolies to unload their stuff, Valerie directing the operation efficiently. As their luggage headed for the far side of the tarmac so did they.

'Right ho, ladies, hope you enjoyed the flight. Very smooth I thought.'

Victoria exchanged a glance with Enid.

'I don't know where you're going next, but no

doubt someone does, and transport will arrive for you eventually.'

The wing co vanished towards the important-looking building on the far side of the airport. She looked around with a grin; well, hardly an airfield, just a strip cut out of the jungle and a few Nissen huts scattered around the edges.

'This is a pretty rotten sort of place, don't you think, Valerie?'

'No worse than I expected, Nester. There's a war on you know. We must expect to be uncomfortable; after all the men are getting shot at as well as enduring these appalling conditions.'

Victoria left the endless inconsequential moaning to the others and sought solitude in the shade. She loved the jungle – its rich fetid smell, the humidity and lushness reminded her of happier times. She dropped her bag on the damp earth and sat on it, just glad to be back on *terra firma*. She was content to wait and let events develop as they would. She had established contact with her parents and even met a man who might prove to be important to her. Was this a turning point in her life? Could she finally move on and be happy again?

ABOUT THE AUTHOR

Fenella J. Miller is a bestselling writer of historical sagas. She also has a passion for Regency romantic adventures and has published over fifty to great acclaim.

Sign up to Fenella J. Miller's mailing list for news, competitions and updates on future books.

Visit Fenella's website: www.fenellajmiller.co.uk

Follow Fenella on social media here:

facebook.com/fenella.miller

x.com/fenellawriter

ALSO BY FENELLA J MILLER

Goodwill House Series

The War Girls of Goodwill House

New Recruits at Goodwill House

Duty Calls at Goodwill House

The Land Girls of Goodwill House

A Wartime Reunion at Goodwill House

Wedding Bells at Goodwill House

A Christmas Baby at Goodwill House

The Army Girls Series

Army Girls: Reporting For Duty

Army Girls: Heartbreak and Hope

Army Girls: Behind the Guns

The Pilot's Girl Series

The Pilot's Girl

A Wedding for the Pilot's Girl

A Dilemma for the Pilot's Girl

A Second Chance for the Pilot's Girl

Victoria's War Series

The Nurse's War

The Nurse's Homecoming

Standalone

The Land Girl's Secret

The Pilot's Story

Sixpence Stories

Introducing Sixpence Stories!

Discover page-turning historical novels from your favourite authors, meet new friends and be transported back in time.

Join our book club
Facebook group

https://bit.ly/SixpenceGroup

Sign up to our
newsletter

https://bit.ly/SixpenceNews

Boldwood

Boldwood Books is an award-winning fiction publishing company seeking out the best stories from around the world.

Find out more at www.boldwoodbooks.com

Join our reader community for brilliant books, competitions and offers!

Follow us
@BoldwoodBooks
@TheBoldBookClub

Sign up to our weekly deals newsletter

https://bit.ly/BoldwoodBNewsletter

www.ingramcontent.com/pod-product-compliance
Lightning Source LLC
Chambersburg PA
CBHW01085713O726
47900CB00017B/2755